'TWAS THE ROGUE BEFORE CHRISTMAS

The Honorable Rogues®
Book Seven

By
COLLETTE CAMERON®

Blue Rose Romance® *LLC*

Sweet-to-Spicy Timeless Romance®

For permission requests, contact the publisher at the email below.

info@collettecameronbooks.com

collettecameronbooks.com
eBook ISBN: 978-1-955259-03-3
Print Book ISBN: 978-1-966087-49-6

. . .

FREE BOOK!

JOIN MY EXCLUSIVE MAILING LIST
Collette Cameron Newsletter

AND GET A FREE EBOOK!

https://collettecameronbooks.com/freegift

Plus Sneak Peeks, Giveaways, Contests, Exclusive Content, and More... P.S. I promise only good stuff ~ **no** spam!

"I doubted true love existed. Until you."

PRAISE FOR...

'TWAS THE ROGUE BEFORE CHRISTMAS

See what readers are saying about
'Twas the Rogue Before Christmas

★★★★★ "An entertaining read with humor, romance, some tender & emotional moments that brought a few tears to my eyes..." ~ Lana Birka

★★★★★ "This book was a quick read, but not lacking at all. I really booked all the characters and the trope was an interesting one." ~ Annglez

★★★★★ "This is a brilliantly written story that is a great addition to this great series. This is a plot that is slightly spicy towards the end, and full of amazing characters. It is a very compelling read that will keep you engaged till the very end." ~ Stephen Williams

. . .

★★★★★ "What a delightful story about Jason and Lenora overcoming the obstacles bent on keeping them apart. I thoroughly enjoyed this sweet tale..." ~ Marti

★★★★★ "I really enjoyed this Book. Collette Cameron has a way to entice & make you fall in love with the characters of her books." ~ AmazingJ

DEDICATION

For every person who appreciates watching others open gifts
more than they enjoy
receiving presents themselves.
Wishing you warmest Christmas blessings.

ONE

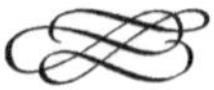

Burlington Arcade
Mayfair, London
28 October 1820

Two years.

Two years and still, Lenora Audsley hadn't entirely adjusted to her new life amongst the upper ten thousand. Hers was the proverbial rags-to-riches fairy tale. From a meager existence in Brighton to a lavish lifestyle amongst the *haut ton*. All thanks to her brother Landry Audsley, Earl of Keyworth, and his persistence in searching for her for eight long years—a half-sister he'd not known existed for the first decade of her life.

Had she wanted to, Lenora couldn't have suppressed the smile curving her mouth as she and her adopted mother, Ruth Smith, and her sister-in-law, Celestia, the Countess of Keyworth, slowly wandered Burlington Arcade's long, elegant passage.

Even the arcade was new and wonderous. All manner of high-end merchants lined either side of the tidy walking lane. Lenora tried not to gawk as she looked from side to side into the large, ornate windows. This was her first visit to the quaint shopping area the upper salons were all abuzz about.

Lenora shook her head at the marvel of it all.

The exclusive, covered market was one of the first of its kind, having been completed the previous March by George Cavendish, Earl of Burlington. Geared toward luxury items and extravagances only the upper crust could afford, Burlington Arcade provided a safer shopping venue for women than Oxford or Bond Streets. Or, truth to tell, the myriad of other fashionable streets the *ton* favored for their shopping excursions.

Usually, Landry insisted at least one footman accompany the women on any outing. Still, he'd acquiesced to his wife's entreating smile when she explained Burlington Arcade was explicitly designed so that women might shop unaccompanied by a male. He'd reluctantly conceded that they might wander Burlington Arcade without Chambers, their burly footman. Nevertheless, Chambers, a former pugilist and reformed street youth, would still accompany them *everywhere* else.

Lenora supposed that was what marriage was about—compromise and concession. Putting your spouse's desires before your own. A willingness to make sacrifices to keep them happy because your loved one's happiness made you glad.

Lenora cut her smiling sister-in-law a side-eyed glance.

Celestia and Landry were so ecstatically content that it was embarrassing at times. Opposites in almost every way; theirs had been a love match. It was quite a romantic tale, in truth.

That had *not* been the relationship between Lenora's adopted parents. Mama believed Lenora ignorant of her father's indiscretions. Or that his last lover, pregnant and enraged, had shoved the vicar down a flight of stairs. Papa had refused to leave Mama and Lenora and make off with the tavern wench. Lenora imagined that as a man of the cloth, even Papa had moral boundaries he wouldn't cross—adultery not being high on that list.

Mama would go to her grave before she discussed the final disgrace that drove them from Lancaster. Still, she must've known the townspeople gossiped—and were careless when a young girl was about. Especially a bashful girl with a tendency to hide amongst the bushes, behind draperies, or under tables and desks where she went unnoticed.

Enough.

Lenora inhaled a purgative breath and purposely returned her focus to the much more pleasant present. Earlier today, she, Mama, and Celestia had visited their modiste, Mademoiselle De la Cour, owner of *Le Belle Haute Couture,* on Bond Street before walking through Burlington Gardens to the Burlington Arcade on this fine autumn day.

Even Mama's cheeks held a rosy tint from the brisk wind that had cleared the skies of coal dust before a sweep of silver-edged clouds once more claimed the heavens as was their wont in late October.

Chambers had placed their packages, including Lenora's exquisite new ballgown for the Wimpletons' Christmastide ball, into the coach and now awaited the women near Burlington Arcade's Piccadilly entrance.

A pair of striking dandies—one wearing a saffron yellow waistcoat and the other a fuchsia and peacock blue striped travesty—approached the trio. The men's gazes lit with masculine interest as they raked their bold perusal over Lenora and Celestia.

Flashing roguish smiles, the young bucks brazenly doffed their hats in Lenora's direction as they passed by. One dared to wink and place his hand over his heart theatrically.

"Hmph," Mama harumphed beneath her breath, prickling like an irate porcupine.

Celestia's family owned a used bookstore—Tolmans' Tomes and Tobacco—and Lenora had read several fascinating books acquired from there. One text discussed animals indigenous to the Americas, including porcupines and a smelly, striped creature called a skunk.

Mama's hand tightened on Lenora's arm as she speared the men with a frosty glare, her lips pinched in disapproval. "Audacious as the devious serpent in the Garden of Eden, the unrepentant rapscallions. I shall pray for their wayward souls."

Once a vicar's wife, always a vicar's wife.

Mama had very stringent ideas about propriety and morality. Gentlemen flirting with a woman they'd not been introduced to most definitely was a black mark against them. Flirting, in general, was frowned upon.

"I fear it cannot be helped, Ruth," Celestia put in with a wide grin and a mischievous wink toward Lenora over the top of Mama's unadorned green bonnet. "Our Lenora is a diamond of the first water. A true original. Men cannot help but be besotted upon seeing her. Landry refused no less than nine offers for her hand last Season and four the previous year."

Lenora had only been aware of six of the proposals. The others Landry must've felt were unsuitable, and the men weren't even given permission to ask her to marry them.

Familiar heat crept up her face. She prayed the shadows from her ocean-blue bonnet and the arched ceiling would hide her blushes. Naturally, she would never admit it aloud—Mama would be scandalized—but Lenora was flattered, even if the masculine attention flustered her somewhat.

What woman didn't enjoy a little harmless admiration?

In truth, she wasn't ready to marry yet. Not when she'd just found her brother. Besides, she loved Celestia like a sister. Eyeing Celestia's rounded tummy, Lenora smiled. No, she wasn't going anywhere until she'd come to know her new nephew or niece.

Regardless, though she knew Celestia meant well, it made Lenora deucedly uncomfortable to be the object of such conjecture. Landry protected her from the worst of the smitten swains with a steely glare or a stern word. He was a most protective brother, and she adored him for it.

Well, most of the time.

On occasion, she wished he'd let her defend herself. She was capable of a smart setdown if the need arose.

Nonetheless, after each social event, numerous flowers arrived along with poems and an assortment of gifts from chocolates to a custom pink quill in its very own ivory velvet case. That novelty had been one of Lenora's favorites. And, of course, the would-be suitors crowded the salon for days afterward.

All of the attention was exhausting and made Lenora feel rather like a mare on the auction block. To be precise, Landry had bestowed a ridiculously generous dowry upon her, and she couldn't be certain her beaux' interest wasn't influenced by her wedding portion.

In point of fact, the Season *was* known as the Marriage Mart. Lenora had endured two Seasons so far, and in truth, preferred the months when the elite fled London for their country estates.

This year, their household hadn't departed for Faringcroft Park, Landry's country seat, due to Celestia's pregnancy. She wanted to be near her family in London when the babe arrived.

Most women preferred the tranquility of country life, but not Celestia. She adored London's hubbub and racket. The bustling activity, the people, *the nonstop energy*, as she called it.

"Lenora is in no hurry to wed," Mama murmured, a trifle

more subdued as they strolled along. Or perhaps she was hopeful that was the case?

Landry had said as much too.

"You'll only marry because you want to, Lenora. You shall have your pick of a husband," he'd said before giving her a fond peck upon the top of her head. "Take your time. I would have you as happily married as I."

Landry had scandalized *le beau monde* by cocking a snook at Society and marrying a commoner. That he was blissfully happy and a powerful lord tempered much of the disapproval. Not all of the censure, however. But then there were always those prepared to judge others.

Neither Landry nor Celestia seemed to care a jot.

"Well, I cannot say I like it," Mama pointed out, leveling another would-be admirer a look that would freeze mangoes off the trees in the Caribbean. Mangoes did not tolerate freezing temperatures—another tidbit Lenora had learned by way of a fascinating book.

"Those scoundrels"—Mama tossed a vexed look over her shoulder—"ought to know better. Ogling young women in such a bold manner. Hmph. They're fortunate the good Lord doesn't smite them for their impure thoughts."

Smite them? Impure thoughts?

The earth would be uninhabited if God went about slaying people for their thoughts.

A vision of purple lightning bolts flashing from the sky and simultaneously striking the men came to mind. Hiding a grin, Lenora quickly turned her head to inspect a picture window display. At least a dozen porcelain dolls ranging in size from six inches to two dolls that stood over four feet tall stared sightlessly back at her.

She hadn't a doubt their cost was very dear. Likely more than a servant made in a year. As a child, she'd always yearned for a beautiful doll with long curly black hair, wearing a ruffled yellow gown and dainty blue slippers. Although money wasn't a concern now, she was too frugal to consider such a triviality.

Besides, what did a grown woman of twenty need with a doll?

Seeking the toy store's signage—*Tippton's Novelties & Nostalgia - Toys for All Ages*—she tucked the name into her memory. She'd need to buy a gift for the baby when it arrived in a few months.

Realizing Celestia had asked her something, Lenora drew her attention away from the display. "I beg your pardon, Celestia. I didn't hear you."

"I asked if you wanted to go inside the toy store," Celestia said.

"No, thank you," Lenora declined. "Perhaps another time."

They neared the arcade's northern entrance.

Celestia smiled at the dapper beadle attired in a top hat and a double-breasted, navy-blue tailcoat adorned with white accents. Two neat rows of six silver buttons, nearly the same shade as the overcast sky, gleamed upon his barrel chest. Brandishing a polished mahogany scepter topped with an ornate silver ball, he held himself with the regal dignity of the loftiest monarch.

Cordially greeting each arriving guest or bidding them farewell, a genial twinkle lit his merry blue eyes. He swept into a flourishing courtier's bow. "Ladies."

Over the top of his broad back, Lenora perused the bustling tableau a few feet away. With a small jolt of alarm, she realized a pair of young, profoundly brazen footpads had set upon an elderly noblewoman and what might've been her lady's maid.

The taller, older blighter viciously shoved the companion

to the ground while the other attempted to wrest the reticule from the lady's frail wrist. The elderly dame wasn't having any of it, however. At once, she began thwacking him with her parasol. The plethora of pink and black feathers adorning her bonnet writhed with each blow she landed.

Not that a parasol was necessary in London in October. An umbrella was most prudent. The lacey accessory did, nevertheless, make a rather admirable weapon.

"Let go, you impudent bounder," the woman demanded in an imperious tone.

Thwack.

"Blighter. Blackguard. Rotter." *Thwack. Thwack.* "Thinking to rob an old lady."

Before Lenora gave a thought to the possible danger or her imprudence for interfering, she sprang into action. She grabbed the flabbergasted beadle's staff and charged at the assailants.

TWO

"Lenora!" Celestia and Mama cried in unison.

"I say, miss," called the astonished beadle behind her. "Come back here with my scepter."

Hadn't he seen the altercation?

Why hadn't he rushed to intervene?

Wasn't that his job?

"What are you doing?" Mama asked in a quavery voice. "You'll get hurt, Lenora."

So might the elderly lady if Lenora did nothing.

"Leave her be." Lenora wacked one thief on his calf hard enough to deter him but not so forceful as to cause him genuine harm.

Howling in pain before unleashing a string of curses that singed Lenora's ears, the robber hopped about on his uninjured leg. "Ye'll pay for that, ye bloody interferin' wench."

Thwack. Thwack. Thwack.

The old woman clobbered her accoster thrice on the shoulder. "Tosspot. Lickspittle. Codpated buggering buffoon."

The woman possessed a rather colorful vocabulary herself.

"Ouch, ye old crone," sneered the thief, batting away the makeshift weapon. "Give me yer money, or I'll plant ye a facer."

"I shall not! I've had a lifetime of males bullying me," she fumed as her colorful bonnet flopped onto her back, and her silvery hair tumbled onto her shoulders. "No more, I say!"

Thwack, thwack to his head.

She was a feisty old bird. Lenora wasn't positive whether she was brave or merely foolhardy.

But as she was jumping into the fray herself, was she so very different?

Landry had warned her of the desperation that drove street youths to rob in broad daylight. Some worked for gangs, but most were simply hungry—starving, in point of fact.

Snarling, the youth raised his fist to strike the old woman as she continued to throttle him with her abused parasol, now a mass of broken sticks.

"Don't you dare hit her, you miscreant," Lenora warned, amazed at her own gumption. She tossed her reticule onto the ground a few feet away. "Take my coin and leave."

At once, his cohort swooped in and, with a gleeful whoop, pocketed the small embroidered velvet bag.

His fellow ruffian laughed, a hollow, half-demented cackle, revealing a broken front tooth amongst his yellowed teeth. "Thank ye kindly, but I'll have hers as well."

He jerked his head toward the woman who was still taking infuriated jabs at him.

It was the hopelessness and beleaguered bleakness in the thief's hardened eyes that stalled Lenora's breath and sent her heartbeat into a syncopated tempo. Unlike herself and the old woman, *he* had nothing to lose.

"My lady," the woman's companion begged in a wavering voice while blinking back tears. "Just give him your purse."

Ah, so the feisty dame *was* nobility. Had the thieves known that? Or was she just an unlucky target because of her age and diminutive size?

Her fraught companion huddled on the pavement, tears streaming down her lined cheeks as she nursed an injured wrist.

"Never," declared the scrappy matron, her eyes narrowed and her puce bonnet hanging askew. She wielded her battered parasol like a saber. "Males who would strike a female are satan's spawns."

She spoke as if she had personal experience.

Fine then.

Lenora would have to deal with the lout. She inched forward, the scepter at the ready.

The second youth faced Lenora, legs braced and a cocky grin skewing his mouth as she bore down upon them. A man shouted something indistinguishable as she brought the staff up to fell the bully attacking the old woman. Using all of her might, she cracked it across his shoulders, sending him reeling and swearing.

"Lenora!" Mama shrieked, terror turning her voice strident.

Cursing foully, the larger thief pulled a wicked-looking knife from his boot.

"No," roared a man from somewhere nearby. "Unhand her."

Finally. Someone else with a backbone and a jot of courage.

Lenora didn't dare turn to see who gave the order with such icy fury and authority.

Fear etched the robber's suddenly waxen face as he dashed a frantic glance around and moved his blade to his other hand.

What stirred such panic in a ruthless cur who'd long since forfeited any integrity or honor?

"Give over yer purse." The first young man wrenched on the woman's reticule again, pulling the matron off balance.

"No. I shan't." She tottered unsteadily, her free arm waving widely.

Lenora instinctively tossed aside the scepter and threw herself in front of the elderly woman. She wrapped her arms around the dame's petite form and rotated so she'd take the brunt of the fall.

Again, she heard her mother and sister-in-law cry out her name.

"*Bloody hell*," a man thundered. "I'll see you in Newgate, you damnable lickspittle."

Lenora's nape prickled at the ferocity.

The words lashed the air with their intensity. It was enough to put the fear of God in everyone witnessing the scene. Mayhap even the curs carrying out their botched robbery.

Bracing her legs, Lenora struggled valiantly to keep herself and the lady upright.

"Let's be off, Janxy," the larger villain growled, his nervous gaze darting over the crowd. "We gots one purse. We still have time to pick a few swells afore the day be over."

The other scraggly thief scanned the crowd for half a second before giving his head a sharp nod.

The footpads dove into the gathering crowd, roughly elbowing people aside in their flight.

"Stop. Thief," a man yelled.

"Catch them," a woman trilled. "Don't let them escape."

Lenora seriously doubted any of the bystanders would attempt to detain a ruffian brandishing a knife with what she perceived as considerable skill.

The aged woman sagged, giving up her attempts to regain her balance.

A fall was imminent.

An instant later, Lenora hit the pavement. Hard. Her hips and shoulders vibrated from the impact before her head snapped back and cracked against the unyielding ground.

Sweet Jesus on Sunday.

A grunt escaped her as the old lady gave a panicked shriek.

The pain nearly crossed Lenora's tear-filled eyes, and she nearly blacked out.

"Grandmother!"

THREE

Outside Burlington Arcade
Mayfair, London

Having spent the past hour perusing booths in Bond Street Bazaar seeking—unsuccessfully—to replace his dagger lost at sea during a skirmish with a pirate, Jason Steele emerged onto Old Bond Street. A helpful merchant had referred him to a skilled knifemaker located within Burlington Arcade.

Given the pleasantness of the day, Jason had opted to walk the short distance. He missed riding, but it was imprudent to stable a horse in London when he was gone so frequently. It wasn't fair to the poor animal. He supposed he could borrow one of his friends' mounts, but Jason didn't like being beholden to anyone.

Without the dagger usually tucked into the waistband of his trousers, he felt oddly naked and vulnerable. Not that he had any worries in this part of London. Unsavory areas such as Whitechapel, Seven Dials, or the rookeries were an entirely different matter.

His father had given him the blade upon his maiden

voyage as *The Arcturus's* captain four years ago. At five-and-twenty, many had thought Jason too young to captain a ship. Nevertheless, his best friend, Ronan Brockman, the son of an English marquess, and Yvette McTavish, the Viscountess Sethwick of Stapleton Shipping and Supplies—the owners of *The Arcturus*—had believed him qualified and capable.

Jason had done his utmost to prove them right, even staving off pirates two weeks ago. Although, to be fair, the ramshackle assortment of swashbucklers and the decrepit ship they manned were scarcely a real threat.

The skirmish had been short with no loss of life of his own crew. The pirates hadn't been as fortunate. The half dozen wounded, motley buccaneers that had scuttled back to their battered vessel like frightened crabs seeking cover would be wise to retire from pillaging on the high seas.

Jason grinned at the memory.

They gave pirating a bad name.

He had been sailing for eleven years by the time he made captain, rising through the ranks from cabin boy to first mate. All of Jason's advancements had been of his own volition, even though he boasted a wealthy and powerful sire. Long ago, he'd learned that achievements gained by one's own endeavors were far more satisfactory than when another paved the way.

Much to his parents' objections and dismay, when war broke out between England and America in 1812, Jason hadn't put aside his obsession with the sea.

He'd been fortunate to avoid direct conflict as he sailed aboard a merchant vessel with an extremely crafty and experienced captain. Captain Connaughton had an instinct for knowing what waters to avoid, and their lengthy journeys to African ports and beyond kept them out of the fray.

Having no interest in taking after his father and delving into the banking industry and politics, Jason would forever be in Brockman's and the viscountess's debt. His four younger brothers, particularly Frank or Owen, might be inclined to follow after Oscar Steele, but Jason most definitely would not. Likely Evan and Thomas wouldn't either.

Some creatures were not meant to be contained, restrained, or confined—to settle down. Most especially to study row upon row of numbers in ledgers within a fusty office, even if it did have a grand view of Boston Harbor. Jason enjoyed his freedom, the comfort of a woman's supple body for mutual pleasure without strings attached, and the ability to go where he wanted when he wanted.

As he maneuvered the busy lane, a few genteel ladies batted their eyelashes and gave him sultry invitations with a simple glance or a seductive peek from beneath their bonnets. Other working-class women not so high in the instep boldly assessed him and, liking what they saw, verbalized as much in blunt terms.

Jason could have his pick of women. He adored women. Adored flirting with them and bringing a blush to their cheeks. Regardless, he was selective with his bed partners. The last thing he wanted was to end up with a case of the clap or the French pox.

Yes indeed, his was an idyllic life.

His grin faltered a fraction.

Or at least it had been until he'd been thrust into the role of...

He scratched his nose and stepped aside for an apple-cheeked nurse pushing a pram containing an infant with impossibly big, blue eyes.

Well, Jason wasn't precisely his maternal grandmother's keeper. The countess would be outraged at the suggestion that anyone needed to mind *her*. She thoroughly enjoyed her newfound liberation and autonomy too much to permit anyone that much control ever again.

Regardless, he felt a responsibility for his grandmother, though it scraped across his independence. He was a free spirit, a wanderer.

His mother, Janelle Steele, had told him as much many times in her cultured British accent when he'd announced that he'd signed on as a cabin boy. "Even as a young boy, I could scarce keep an eye on you, Jason. You were always taking off and exploring. Nothing kept your attention for long."

Another grin tipped his mouth upward at the corners as he recalled his petite mother wrangling her five sons under control with nothing more than a stern glance and a softly voiced reprimand. She was so different from their big, blustery, loud, rough-around-the-edges American father. Proof that opposites do attract and, in his parents' case, could make a splendid match.

It was too bad Mama had only birthed sons. She would have to be content with her daughters-in-law. *If* and when any of the Steele brothers wed.

Whistling a sailing ditty, "Whisky O," as he strode along earned Jason several reproving stares from elitist Londoners but appreciative grins from the commoners. The British thought whistling crass. But as he didn't give a buffalo's rump what the English thought about him, he continued to warble, even singing a line or two beneath his breath.

In truth, he was sorely tempted to imitate several bird calls he'd mastered over the years just to see the pompous Brits' reactions. A barn owl's screech might prove highly amusing. Many thought the sound otherworldly or demonic. If one didn't know what the eerie noise was, it did raise one's nape hairs.

As Jason approached the Burlington Arcade's north

entrance, he furrowed his brow. He had a bit of a conundrum. Grandmother Darlington-Pope expected he'd stay with her in London for at least two months before he sailed again. Given his current sailing schedule, he'd believed that as well.

Nonetheless, just yesterday, a prosperous proposition had been put to him by Ronan Brockman that meant an extended voyage to depart before Christmas. Six months away at sea, at least. More likely eight or nine.

Jason's best friend, Ronan, no longer joined him on *The Arcturus.* They'd met aboard the ship and formed a bond closer than brothers in the few years they'd sailed together.

But Ronan had lost his head a couple of years ago. He'd fallen in love and married, and now he wouldn't consider leaving his wife for months on end.

Jason supposed some men were content with that domesticated life. Many, in truth. It simply had never been a desire of his. The world was large and fascinating, and there was so much he wanted to see.

If he accepted the assignment, he'd also be letting his mother down. He'd promised to spend the time while *The Arcturus* was in dry dock for maintenance with her mother, Adalia, the Dowager Countess Darlington-Pope. Still, the chance to captain one of Stapleton Shipping and Supplies' other ships for the anticipated voyage to India was an opportunity he hated to pass up.

It was a high honor indeed.

But there was his aging grandmother to consider.

Halbert Glenister, Earl of Darlington-Pope, had died a year and a half ago. A distant cousin had inherited the title. Jason had never met the old coot nor the new earl. What he little he knew of his deceased grandfather was what his mother had told him, and nothing she'd said flattered the crusty curmudgeon.

Grandfather had disinherited her after she'd married an American without the earl's permission. The vengeful and bitter rotter had also forbidden his countess to communicate with their only child.

Now, with her year of mourning behind her, Grandmother was like an animal released from its cage for the first time. She'd secretly written to her daughter all of those years and was determined to make up for the time she'd been under her husband's oppressive thumb.

A commotion in front of Burlington Arcade snared Jason's attention.

Narrowing his eyes, he automatically reached for his knife. His fingers met empty air instead of a familiar smooth elk antler handle, and he cursed beneath his breath.

Bugger and blast.

It appeared a pair of street ruffians were attempting a robbery in broad daylight. No sly nimble-fingered pickpocket tricks either. One brazenly wrenched at an elderly lady's reticule as she pummeled him with her parasol.

Wait.

Jason's heartbeat increased into a gallop, and something the size and weight of a cannonball throttled to his throat where his Adam's apple ought to have been.

Hell's bells. It's Grandmother.

FOUR

Why was Grandmother alone?

Where was Fellowes, her coachman?

Jason's gaze snagged on a forlorn figure wearing muted blue and huddled on the ground. Not alone, then. Nonetheless, Myrtle Grayson was practically as old as Grandmother and not nearly as spry.

Even as Jason broke into a sprint, a young woman dashed toward his grandmother from the other direction. Without hesitation, she clobbered one villain with a stick of some sort, then turned on the other assailant.

Despite the seriousness of the situation, a dry chuckle escaped him.

A regular firebrand.

Jason hadn't known they existed in England.

Her marine-blue redingote swirled about her ankles, and her bonnet's ribbons came undone as she whirled around to confront the second thug. The frilly accessory flew from her head, revealing a halo of burnished red curls.

A firebrand with fiery red hair.

Unfortunately, her bravado had only succeeded in further enraging the thieves.

Jason picked up his pace, breaking into a run and shouting for people to clear a path. They darted to the sides, complaining or letting out little cries of confusion and alarm.

One of the youths now brandished an evil blade. From the deft way he shifted it from hand to hand, he was no novice with the weapon.

Devil and damn.

Of all of the times to be without his own blade. Still, a pair of callow youths were no match for him. Particularly when they were stupid enough to attack his not-so-frail grandmother.

At that moment, she landed a hardy blow on her attacker's shoulder.

Bully for you, Grandmother.

Jason never would've believed the diminutive woman capable of such feistiness.

The young woman continued to defend his grandmother while other passersby shied away. Not so far that they couldn't retain their excellent view of the altercation, however. Even the men, the dandified coxcombs, slunk backward. The portly beadle who was supposed to guard Burlington Arcade's entrance hovered behind the crowd, peeking over the spectators' shoulders.

Lilly-livered poltroons all.

Jason owed the young woman a debt of gratitude for her bravery and fortitude.

His grandmother's protector's brilliant coppery hair had tumbled from her neat chignon and swung about her shoulders and back as she waved the stick she held. No, not a stick. There was something shiny on one end.

As he neared the ruckus, the lout yanking on his grandmother's reticule pulled her off balance. The roaring in Jason's ears and the blood humming through his veins deafened him to what he shouted at the thugs. He'd reached the onlookers but couldn't get to his grandmother in time to prevent her tumble.

"I'll see you in prison," Jason roared.

To his utter astonishment, the young redhead hurled herself in front of Grandmother. She gripped his grandmother in a tight embrace and then twisted her agile young body so that she would hit the pavement first.

After a panicked glance at Jason's incensed countenance, the thieves wisely turned tail and fled.

Just as he reached his grandmother, she and the young woman toppled to the ground.

Grandmother cried out.

In pain?

"Grandmother?" Jason whispered, falling to his knees beside them both and tentatively touching his grandmother's narrow back. "Grandmother?" he said again when she didn't respond.

"Lenora," wailed a woman stumbling to a stop beside him, dragging the name out into several extra syllables.

Another woman rushed to their sides as well.

Glancing upward, Jason pulled his eyebrows together.

The Countess of Keyworth?

Yes, Keyworth's wife.

Jason had met her at some event or other.

"Jason?"

His grandmother's warbly voice dragged his attention back to her.

"Yes, Grandmother. Are you hurt?" He put a staying hand on her shoulder when she tried to roll over. "Don't move until I'm sure you are fine."

"Pshaw. I'm going to bruise like a plum, my boy. There's no doubt about that nor preventing it either."

No small amount of truth there.

Pushing onto one elbow, she turned her head to look at him. "But this poor dear is truly hurt, I fear." She waved a gnarled hand in his direction. "Help me to sit, my boy. We must see to my savior at once. I've already sent for my coach. I cannot imagine why Fellowes hasn't arrived as yet."

A pale-faced beadle rushed forward, now that the danger had passed. After collecting his abused scepter, he asked the Countess of Keyworth, "How may I be of service, my lady?"

"Please send a boy to have my coach brought around to this side of the arcade." The Countess of Keyworth's attention never veered from the redhead sprawled on the pavement.

"At once, my lady." With a dip of his head, the beadle bustled away. With a practiced flick of his wrist, he signaled to a young lad of perhaps ten or twelve years of age loitering near the entrance.

Poor lad. He'd likely never be permitted to enter Burlington Arcade.

After a brief exchange, the boy nodded and dashed away, his thin legs churning.

"Lenora?" The white-faced woman whispered again, her horrified eyes wide as she stared at the pale-as-chalk girl prone on the ground. She seemed incapable of uttering anything else.

Dark umber lashes the same shade as her winged eyebrows fanned the girl's pale cheeks as she lay unmoving. Dark crimson blood seeped from beneath her head.

"Handkerchiefs," announced Lady Keyworth matter of factly. "I need handkerchiefs at once."

Without waiting for the gawkers to procure their handkerchiefs, she stuck her hand out and demanded the onlookers hand over the scraps. Several gentlemen and ladies readily complied.

Sure.

Now that the danger had passed, the bystanders had become all helpful solicitousness. The cowards would most likely embellish their tales later and portray themselves as Good Samaritans for assisting a woman in distress.

Regardless, Jason also offered his tidily folded handkerchief.

The countess kneeled beside Lenora and, gently lifting her head, pressed the cloths to her scalp. "Darling, can you hear me? Open your eyes, Lenora. Please, dear."

Lenora's lashes fluttered, and she opened her eyes.

Her turquoise gaze collided with Jason's, and double mule kicks to the gut couldn't have rendered him less able to breathe. He'd never seen eyes that color, like the deepest, most transparent ocean but rimmed with dark forest green.

She stared back at him, a puzzled look of wonderment in her gaze. "Do I know you? I feel as if I must."

She'd felt that instant connection too, even in her sorry state?

Smiling gently, Jason shook his head. When a shock of hair fell over his forehead, he realized he'd lost his hat somewhere as he'd pelted to his grandmother's aid. He had no doubt the expensive Oxonian was long gone. Probably already bartered by a street urchin for a loaf of bread.

The British thought all Americans were uncouth bumpkins. He might as well prove them right by introducing himself and Grandmother. "We've not been introduced. I'm Captain Jason Steele, and the woman you aided is my grandmother, the Dowager Countess of Darlington-Pope."

"Oh," Lenora whispered.

Evidently, the Countess of Keyworth and the distraught

woman at her side were too overwrought to introduce themselves. Or perhaps they thought him presumptuous and simply refused to do Jason the same courtesy.

Drawing her eyebrows together, Lenora winced. "Are they gone?"

No need to ask who *they* were.

"Yes, dear," the Countess of Keyworth assured her. "The curs fled moments ago. You were very brave, Lenora."

"Hear, hear," a man called from the semi-circle of spectators. "She's a veritable Artemisia."

"I think the whole display was vulgar and unbecoming," a woman sniffed, her tone haughty and condescending.

"Ye wouldn't be sayin' that if she'd saved *ye* from a robbery," intoned another man.

Lady Keyworth squeezed Lenora's hand, then folded the handkerchiefs and applied the bloodied cloths to Lenora's head once more. "Your brother will be so very proud."

"I doubt it." A grimace crossed Lenora's ashen face. "Landry will call me foolhardy and reckless."

The injured beauty was Keyworth's sister?

Why hadn't Jason known that?

In point of fact, he didn't travel in the same circles as the Keyworths. In general, Jason avoided *ton* gatherings. He disliked being dissected by snobs and having his failings publicly cataloged, including his American origins.

Jason removed his neckcloth and passed it wordlessly to the Countess of Keyworth.

Somewhere behind him, a woman gasped in rapt astonishment. "I cannot countenance it. Why, he's actually disrobing in public."

"He's an American," a man remarked as if that explained Jason's indecorous behavior.

The Countess of Keyworth gave him a grateful smile as

she gingerly wrapped the length of fabric around Lenora's head.

"Indeed, you were courageous, my dear. I owe you a tremendous thanks," Grandmother said, patting Lenora's hand.

"My head hurts," Lenora murmured as her eyelashes fluttered closed once more.

Had she fainted?

A coach drew up. Grim-faced, Grandmother's driver hopped down.

"What has happened, my lady?" Fellowes asked, lines of worry etched into his already craggy features. Myrtle and Grandmother still sat upon the ground. At once, Fellowes helped both women to their feet.

Grandmother met Jason's gaze. "Jason, do lift Lenora into my coach at once. She requires medical attention. Perhaps even stitches." She glanced up. "Lady Keyworth. Have you a preferred physician we should send for? If not, I can recommend mine."

"We do." Lady Keyworth motioned to the beadle, who rushed to her side again. She passed him a few coins. "Have a lad fetch my physician, John Calder, on Cowley Street. Tell the doctor to come to Keyworth House straightaway."

"Yes, my lady." The beadle scrambled to do as bid, and soon another lad took off toward Cowley Street.

Without waiting for permission from the countess or the other eagle-eyed woman he'd begun to suspect was Lenora's mother, Jason scooped Lenora into his arms.

Instantly, her eyelids popped open, and her nostrils flared.

She was a slight little thing. Not exactly petite in stature, but by no means did she harbor any excessive weight.

"I *can* walk, Captain Steele," she informed him in a prim tone that made his lips twitch.

"I don't doubt that you can, but I don't believe it would be wise until a physician examines you."

She sliced his grandmother, who now soothed her distraught lady's maid, a side-eyed glance as he strode to the waiting coach. Beneath her breath, she asked, "Are you always so bossy, Captain Steele?"

Grinning, Jason winked. "Only, it seems, Miss Audsley, when it comes to you."

"Lucky me," she muttered tartly before deliberately closing her eyes and turning her face away.

He'd guessed correctly. She *was* Keyworth's sister.

"No, lucky me," Jason murmured for her ears alone.

Very, very lucky indeed.

FIVE

On the way to Keyworth House
Mayfair, London
A short while later

Lenora kept her eyes closed on the coach ride home and concentrated on not casting up her accounts. She lay upon one seat, and Mama, Jason Steele, and the Dowager Countess of Darlington-Pope sat crammed together on the opposite.

Celestia and Lady Darlington-Pope's abigail had awaited the arrival of the Keyworths' coach after the lad had been sent to notify the driver to come around to the other side of Burlington Arcade.

"Do not fall asleep, Miss Audsley, though I know it is tempting," Captain Steele repeated for at least the sixth or seventh time.

Bossy.

How does he know anyway?

Had he been cracked upon the noggin?

"A physician needs to examine you first," he reiterated again.

He was a ship's captain, which undoubtedly explained his commanding presence and why he felt he could order her about and expect prompt compliance.

"Miss Audsley?" he persisted, more annoying than a fly buzzing over teatime dainties or stinging ants at a picnic.

"I'm awake, Captain," Lenora responded, though the effort to open her eyes was too great.

In truth, sleep sounded utterly splendid. However, she'd hit the back of her head, and the risk of concussion was real. At present, Captain Steele's neckcloth served as a bandage wrapped around her head to hold the pilfered handkerchiefs in place.

She must look an utter fright.

Lenora couldn't bring herself to care a whit.

Mama had been peculiarly silent except when Captain Steele had lifted Lenora into his arms with the ease of a child picking up a kitten.

"I am Lenora's mother, Ruth Smith, and I shall accompany you to Keyworth House, Captain Steele," she'd announced in a no-nonsense tone.

Mama had never taken up her actual name of Smythe-Shufflebottom after Papa's perfidy. Not that Lenora blamed her in the least. She had reason to be angry and resentful. Papa's behavior was untenable, especially for a man of God who regularly preached morality from the pulpit.

Do as I say and not as I do seemed to be his doctrine.

"Naturally, you must accompany us, Mrs. Smith," Lady Darlington-Pope had agreed, wincing slightly as her coachman handed her into the waiting conveyance. "You must be so proud of your daughter's courage."

Mama made a noncommittal sound in her throat as the coachman assisted her inside.

Proud mightn't be the best terminology to describe Mama's sentiments. She loathed dramatics and ostentatious emotional displays. More on point, she despised her own loss of self-control. She prided herself on her restraint during taxing situations and to have shrieked Lenora's name, not once, but twice in public...

Likely she was wallowing in self-recrimination.

To a small degree, Lenora was as well.

She disliked upsetting her mother. Likely, Mama was more upset that Lenora had put herself in harm's way than her unseemly public behavior. She mightn't have given birth to Lenora, but no biological mother could be more devoted or love her daughter more.

Lenora had never known her own mother. Consequently, she didn't miss the woman who'd given birth to her. Nevertheless, that lady, the now-deceased Countess of Keyworth, had loved her, Landry had told Lenora.

She'd not relinquished Lenora willingly, but as Lenora was the result of a love affair, the previous earl had made arrangements for Mama and Papa to raise her. All without the countess's knowledge or consent.

Upon her deathbed, the Countess of Keyworth had confided in her son, and Landry had spent the next eight years looking for Lenora. Only back then, she'd gone by the name Laureen. Mama hadn't asked why she and her husband were given a tiny days-old babe, but she suspected the truth would be unsavory. Prudently, she'd changed Lenora's name.

After Landry's investigator had located her, and she'd learned who she was, Lenora changed her name to the one her birth mother had given her. Mama hadn't minded. She said it was the least Lenora could do to honor the poor woman who'd had her infant daughter stolen from her.

Cracking an eyelid open, Lenora looked straight into Captain Steele's probing hazel-eyed gaze. His thick-lashed, navy-blue rimmed irises were the color of the sky before a storm, she decided somewhat nonsensically, considering her present circumstances. No man should have eyes that beautiful. They mesmerized and held one captive, helpless to look away.

She'd never before had cause to ponder a gentleman's eye color, and that she did this stranger's struck her as incongruous. Raised by a strictly religious mother, Lenora had little opportunity to romanticize anything. Mama discouraged such fanciful ponderings as vain imaginations.

Regardless, Lenora found her focus trained on Captain Steele's handsome face. Those same beguiling eyes crinkled at the corners as he offered a reassuring tilt of his firm mouth. His face was unusually sun-kissed, a silent testament to long hours spent outdoors.

London's fops and dandiprats were insipid lilies compared to Captain Steele.

"Feeling better?" he asked in a deliciously deep rumbling timbre, his arms folded across his broad chest.

"Yes," Lenora admitted truthfully.

She was. For certain, her head was sore where she'd hit the pavement, but other than that and a queasy stomach brought on by the carriage's lurching motion, she was fine.

Captain Steele possessed an odd accent she hadn't heard before. She suspected he might be an American. She'd always heard they were monstrous, bearded, uncouth men. However, the striking, wide-shouldered, sable-haired gentleman relaxing across from her might've been an English nobleman.

Except...

There was a glint in Captain Jason Steele's eyes, turning

them from hazel to a steely gray. She liked how his eyes changed color. There was a confident, devil-may-care aura about him. A cock-a-snook at strictures and protocol mien as if he didn't honestly give two farthings what anyone thought of him.

In truth, Lenora would be bound he didn't.

Of its own accord, her dratted focus drifted to his bare throat, where a very masculine Adam's apple was on full display in a corded neck thanks to his sacrificing his neckcloth for an improvised bandage.

Lord, she must look a fright, Lenora thought again as heat swept up her cheeks. Most annoying since she rarely colored or blushed. Good thing too. With her startling red hair, she resembled a pomegranate when she colored.

"Might I sit up?" Lenora asked, placing a palm upon her middle. "The coach's jostling is wreaking havoc upon my stomach."

Vehicle rides had always made her ill unless she sat facing forward. In this prone position, she rather felt like a helpless cork bobbing upon the high seas.

"Of course." At once, Mama crouched in the middle of the coach and helped Lenora to a sitting position.

Surprisingly, her head didn't swim, and she wasn't the least dizzy. That boded very well indeed. Likely, no concussion then. Only an abrasion at the back of her head, which stung like the dickens.

After Mama had settled beside her, Lady Darlington-Pope scooted to the other side of her bench. "There you are, Jason. You can spread out now. I know you've been cramped."

At once, he unfolded from his hunched position and took up three-quarters of the seat.

A ping of guilt jabbed Lenora. While she'd enjoyed an

entire bench, the others had been jammed upon the opposite seat like sardines in a tin.

Mama tucked Lenora's hand into her own. She gave Lenora's fingers a little squeeze. "You frightened a decade off of me, darling."

Her voice turned raspy, and she cleared her throat while blinking rapidly.

Lenora didn't miss the sheen of tears in her mother's eyes.

"I'm sorry, Mama." Lenora sent Lady Darlington-Pope a sideways glance and a weak half-smile. "I simply couldn't stand by and do nothing."

"Grateful I am too, Miss Audsley. You dealt those bounders a hefty blow or two." Lady Darlington-Pope beamed back at her. Though she had to be past her seventieth year, except for fine lines framing her eyes and mouth and two wrinkles etched upon her forehead, her ladyship's face remained remarkably smooth.

There was a resemblance around her eyes and aristocratic cheekbones that portrayed Captain Steele as her grandson.

Lenora could have stood by, of course, and declined to intervene. Just as everyone else had. The truth was, she had surprised even herself. Nonetheless, she didn't regret her actions.

She was convinced Lady Darlington-Pope would've been injured had she not intervened. The woman was mulishly stubborn, and nothing short of bodily harm would've forced her to give over her money.

What was it she'd said?

"I've been bullied by men all of my life." Or something of that nature.

Head resting against the plush royal blue velvet squabs, Lenora studied Captain Steele from beneath her eyelashes.

Was *he* one of the bullies her ladyship had referred to?

No, his grandmother looked at him with doting fondness. And from the affectionate glances he sent her every now and again, the sentiment was mutual.

Lenora's musings turned inward as she considered the repercussions of her impulsiveness. For undoubtedly, there would be consequences. Whether they would take the form of censure and ostracism, or whether she'd be heralded as heroic, only time would tell.

The upper ten thousand were a fickle lot. The oddest thing might take their fancy and be heralded as fashionable, and a simple *faux pas* could result in the cut direct.

A few minutes later, the coach drew to a halt before Keyworth House. Captain Steele didn't wait for the footman to open the door. He leaned his large, muscular form forward and pressed the latch before nimbly leaping to the ground.

Lenora couldn't help but notice how the fabric of his superfine black wool coat pulled taut across his back at the movement. Or the way the muscles in his gray-clad thighs bunched and rippled. The man assuredly wasn't a soft-bellied coxcomb.

No, everything about Captain Jason Steele shouted raw, untamed masculinity—alluring and alarming. A juxtaposition of attraction and leeriness cascaded over her. She wrinkled her forehead. Perhaps she'd hit her head harder than she'd thought, for what other sensible reason could there be for her absurd mental ramblings?

Two footmen descended the house stairs, one heading to their coach and one to the conveyance that had pulled up directly behind them. That would be Celestia and Lady Darlington-Pope's maid.

Once Mama and her ladyship had been handed down from the equipage, Lenora scooted to the edge of the seat. She stood at the entrance and extended her hand toward Captain

Steele. She wasn't dizzy, but she also wasn't foolish enough to try to descend unaided. Another tumble today was not desirable.

A little yelp of surprise escaped her when Captain Steele swept her into his arms again without a word of warning.

SIX

Keyworth House entry

The opportunistic bounder!

The first time the captain had lifted her, Lenora had been so befuddled, she hadn't noticed the solid wall of his chest pressing into her or the iron-like grip of his arms beneath her shoulder and thighs.

This time, she was very much aware.

He smelled good too—soap and bayberry and mayhap mint.

A slight shadow covered his angular jaw and neck. From her position, she caught sight of curly black hair peeking from the vee of his shirt. Her body reacted most peculiarly, coming alive as awareness sang along her veins, and her pulse took on a new, accelerated tempo.

Lenora was afraid to meet anyone's gazes lest they see the wantonness in hers. For surely that was what it must be.

What other explanation was there?

She'd only just met this man—*he's held you in his arms*

twice. She couldn't possibly feel anything for him except gratitude.

Perhaps she was concussed after all.

Yes, yes, that explained her irregular reaction.

Keyworth House's butler, Teeven, a former prizefighter, stood at the entrance. His hawkish eyebrows wrestled with each other above an obviously many times broken nose as he took in the scene.

"Teeven, Doctor Calder should be here shortly." Untying her stylish bonnet, Celestia hurried up the steps with an alacrity her rounded tummy contradicted.

Teeven's astute gaze swept over those behind her.

"Please show him to Lenora's chamber immediately," Celestia said. "There's been an accident."

"So I see, my lady," he intoned in his gruff voice. He always sounded like he'd gargled nails for breakfast. Landry said it was because he'd taken an almost lethal blow to the throat during a boxing match that permanently damaged his vocal cords.

Glancing behind her as she removed her bonnet, Celestia said, "He'll also need to examine the Countess of Darlington-Pope and her lady's maid. They'll need chambers to refresh themselves and rest in. Please have tea and a light repast brought to them too."

"Of course, my lady." Teeven signaled a pair of maids awaiting his direction. One promptly tore upstairs, and the other made directly for the kitchen.

The footmen were assisting Lady Darlington-Pope and her lady's maid up the entry stairs much more slowly. Looking worse for wear, the aged women leaned heavily upon the solicitous servants' arms.

"I assure you, Captain Steele, I *am* quite capable of walking," Lenora said a bit more tartly than she'd intended to hide her discomfit and chagrin. She detested being the focus of unwanted attention.

And yet you took a stick to two thieves in broad daylight outside a posh establishment.

That was different, she argued to herself. *Lady Darlington-Pope required assistance and no one else seemed the least inclined.*

"Captain," she said between her teeth. "I *can* walk."

He shifted her in his arms, causing an undefinable sensation to sluice through her.

"We shall let the physician make that determination," he murmured, effortlessly climbing the stairs behind the others.

"Obstinate man," she muttered beneath her breath, uncharacteristically cross.

"Only when it comes to you, it seems, Miss Audsley."

Captain Steele flashed a wide grin as they passed the worried butler and nodded a friendly greeting.

"How do you do?" he asked the flabbergasted majordomo. "I'm Captain Jason Steele of Boston, Massachusetts." He indicated Lenora with a dip of his angular chin. "There was a robbery."

"I...see." Teeven blinked several times before clearing his throat. "I am well, Captain Steele." Recovering from his shock, the servant swept a troubled glance over Lenora, lingering on the bloody bandage encasing her head. "You are injured, miss?"

Concern puckered his already contorted countenance.

"Not seriously," Lenora assured him, waving a hand toward the back of her head. "Just a little knock on my head when I tumbled onto the pavement. Head wounds tend to bleed profusely."

Another morsel she'd gleaned from a book acquired at Tolmans' Tomes and Tobacco.

"We do not yet know the extent of your injuries," Jason countered.

"*I know*," Lenora muttered peevishly.

She glared at his sharply hewn jawline, and despite her annoyance with him, wondered how rough the bristles would feel beneath her fingertips.

Or lips.

Good Lord on Sunday.

Whatever had taken her thoughts down that unholy path?

Lenora purposefully focused on Captain Steele's disregard of her wishes. She did not like his highhandedness nor his dismissing her protests with little more care than swatting away an annoying mosquito. For good measure and to show her displeasure, she jabbed him in the ribs with her elbow.

His grunt as the appendage hit home caused the edges of her mouth to twitch in satisfaction. Until now, Lenora had lamented her bony elbows. However, they'd just proved themselves immensely useful, and never again would she bemoan the knobby joints.

"Bloodthirsty little thing, aren't you, minx?" Captain Steele murmured near her ear as concerned maids—not a one above fifteen years in age because Landry only hired street youths—appeared and directed his grandmother and her companion toward the grand staircase.

"Only when it comes to you, Captain, it seems," Lenora retorted with a syrupy sweet, disingenuous smile.

That much was true. Usually, she possessed a congenial, patient, and kind nature.

He gave her an exaggerated long-suffering look. "Alas, what I must suffer for chivalry's sake."

Mama turned to them. A hint of impatience shadowed her typically placid features as she gestured insistently for Captain Steele to follow her. "This way, if you please, Captain Steele."

He aimed them toward the stairs.

And halted.

Landry stood three risers from the bottom, his jaw tight and his keen gaze surveying the chaotic foyer.

How long had he been standing there?

His attention settled on Lenora cradled against Captain Steele's chest. The corners of her brother's eyes flexed, and his nostrils flared.

He was angry. Truly angry.

The occurrence was so rare that Lenora stiffened in Captain Steele's arms and made a distressed sound in the back of her throat. Surely Landry had seen the makeshift bandage encircling her head and deduced she'd been injured.

Or perhaps, her brother wasn't capable of rational thought at the moment.

She made another distraught noise that sounded to her ears suspiciously like a whimper.

Lenora did not whimper.

"Shh," Jason murmured, tightening his embrace for a heartbeat. "It's all right, Lenora," he soothed, his voice barely audible.

"Please do explain why my sister is in your arms, *Steele*," Landry drawled, slow and dangerous.

That wasn't good. No indeed.

When it came to protecting Lenora, Landry would strike first and ask questions later. Truthfully, he couldn't very well plant Jason a facer when he carried her. But the instant Jason put her down...?

Did Jason have any idea how much danger he was in?

She must do something.

Now.

But what?

Her mind frantically foraged around for a solution.

A fit of the vapors?

Yes. Yes. That was perfect.

Never mind that Lenora had never succumbed to a swoon in her life.

Turning her face into Jason's chest, she whispered, "I'm going to pretend to faint."

His gaze careened to hers, a question in the warm—*amused?*—depths of his eyes. He speared a guarded glance toward Landry, then returned his regard to her and crooked a sable eyebrow.

"Play along." She winked her left eye, confident no one could see her as that side of her face lay against him.

Comprehension registered, and his mouth parted as if to refute her.

Stupid man.

He assuredly did not want Landry for an enemy. True, her brother possessed a tender heart toward street urchins, but there was nothing softhearted about him when it came to protecting his family.

There was nothing for it then. She must fake a faint.

Men could be so utterly obtuse.

For the first time in her life, and to protect a man she didn't know from her brother's wrath, Lenora slumped into a full-on swoon.

Her collapse must've been believable, for a maid gasped, "Miss Lenora!"

"Oh dear," Cecelia murmured.

"Heavens above. She's fainted dead away." Mama's voice emerged on a strangled croak. "Lord, touch my daughter with thine healing hand," she prayed haltingly. "Hurry, Captain Steele. Carry her upstairs at once."

"Of course," Jason murmured, the merest hint of laughter tinging the two words.

"Oh, where is the doctor?" Mama practically wailed.

Lenora prayed everyone would take the slight quiver in Captain Steele's voice for concern and not hilarity, which she was positive was the real cause of his unsteady timbre. If she didn't risk discovery, she'd have pinched him.

She still might if the opportunity arose.

"Up the stairs, Captain Steele. To your right. Third door on the left." Celestia calmly gave him the directions to Lenora's bedchamber.

"My goodness," cried Lady Darlington-Pope in a quavering tone. "I do hope Miss Audsley is not seriously injured. I'll never forgive myself."

"Please do not trouble yourself, Grandmother," Jason said as he continued to the staircase. "I'd wager my ship that Miss Audsley's recovery is nearly miraculous in nature."

He was definitely laughing at her, the *roué*.

How badly Lenora wanted to pinch him. Nonetheless, she'd put them in this delicate situation, and she'd suffer a slightly bruised pride if it spared her brother calling Jason out.

"I'll send Doctor Calder up as soon as he arrives," Teeven assured no one in particular.

He retraced his passage to the entrance. The unmistakable sound of the front door opening declared he intended to accost the poor physician the instant he drew up before Keyworth House.

"Will somebody please tell me what the hell is going on?" Landry thundered. "What has happened to my sister? Steele? Celestia? *Anyone?*"

Lenora imagined Landry's gaze impaling Jason, then swinging to his wife before careening around the foyer.

Guilt stabbed her at her brother's genuine worry.

Mama's and Celestia's as well.

She'd only carry on with this charade a minute or two

more. As soon as she was in her room and the danger of her overwrought brother doing something foolhardy had passed, she'd awaken from her fit of the vapors and assure everyone she was perfectly fine.

A miraculous recovery indeed.

"I'll let your lady fill you in on the details," Jason murmured a trifle too jocularly as he mounted the stairs and passed Landry.

Something very near a growl reverberated in Landry's throat.

Lenora fought to remain immobile and keep her features relaxed. It was wholly unnatural, and a deplorable urge to giggle began in her belly and continued up to her throat.

It was rather like when one had an itch in an unmentionable place that grew worse the more one contemplated it. Or perhaps, she mused, it was more like a tickle in one's throat during a sermon or a musical that could only be alleviated by a robust round of coughing.

"Her room's just here," Mama said rather breathlessly as if she'd sprinted up the stairs. The creak of a door opening met Lenora's ears. "Please lay her on the bed."

What else would he do?

Drop Lenora unceremoniously onto the floor?

A handful of seconds later, Jason gently lowered her to her comfortable mattress. Hopefully, her lovely emerald sea foam green and ivory counterpane wouldn't become bloodstained.

"Thank you," he whispered into her ear. "It wasn't necessary to protect me."

That little rush of desire, as soft as butterflies' wings, whisked over her again.

Get a hold of yourself, Lenora Esther Elizabeth Audsley.

"What's that you are saying to her?" Mama asked before the bed sank on Lenora's other side.

Lenora well knew the starchy look Mama no doubt pinned him with.

"I told her I'd say a prayer for a full and swift recovery," Jason lied as smoothly as any practiced charlatan.

It was precisely the right thing to say to earn Mama's approval, however. As he probably suspected. *The colossal, disarming liar.*

"Oh. Yes. Please do." Her mother cleared her throat and pressed a cool palm to Lenora's forehead. "Prayers would be much appreciated. I have always believed in the power of prayer."

"I'm *positive* your daughter shall be right as rain in no time, Mrs. Smith," Jason reassured her. His voice was smooth and comforting. The tone one used to calm a skittish puppy or horse. "She's young and healthy."

Gratitude warmed Lenora that he should make an effort to console her mother.

"But there was so much blood," Mama murmured in a muffled voice. Had she put her handkerchief to her mouth to stifle a sob?

"Head wounds always bleed profusely." He shifted, jostling the mattress. "See this? I acquired it a fortnight ago during a scuffle with a pirate. It bled something awful, but I didn't even suffer a headache afterward."

Pirate? Lord above.

She'd considered that the wives of sea captains must be lonely and independent too, as their husbands could be gone for years at a time. But Lenora hadn't honestly contemplated the dangers apart from foul weather.

She bit the inside of her cheek to keep from looking at whatever mark he indicated to her mother. At last, she could stand it no longer. She opened her eyes just as the bewhiskered doctor whisked through the doorway, worn leather satchel in hand.

Landry was directly on his heels with thunder in his eyes.

Drat and double drat.

Her ploy hadn't worked after all.

"I hear you've had a bit of excitement today, Miss Audsley." Doctor Calder eyed her head with its neckcloth bandage. "Let's have a look, shall we?"

"Yes, and while Doctor Calder examines my sister, you and I shall have a discussion in my study, Steele." Landry's tone was as hard and unyielding as forged steel.

SEVEN

Keyworth House study
A few tense minutes later

Wordlessly and without preamble, the Earl of Keyworth ushered Jason into the study. An enormous shaggy black dog rose to his feet, his long, bushy tail waving tentatively as he looked between his master and Jason.

"Stay, Sampson," Keyworth said, holding his palm outward.

The dog promptly sank onto the hearth.

"Lie down. There's a good boy."

Sampson released a hearty sigh, licked his chops a couple of times, then rested his head upon his giant paws.

Jason liked dogs and would've petted Sampson, but given Keyworth's less than affable attitude, he decided against the overture.

Upon closing the door behind them, Keyworth directed Jason to one of two overstuffed royal-blue damask armchairs arranged at angles before a tidy desk. Likely his wife's influence. Landry, no doubt, would likely have chosen stiff leather chairs to discourage visitors from lingering overly long.

A brass, chariot-shaped inkwell and quill holder sat perfectly centered atop the glossy desktop. That would be Keyworth's doing. Everything orderly—right down to who was permitted to carry his injured sister.

"Have a seat," Keyworth said in clipped tones with a terse sweep of his hand.

It wasn't a request.

Typical of British nobility.

Aristocrats gave orders and expected everyone to obey at once. Only, Jason was a proud American, and he didn't bloody well care if Keyworth believed himself superior to a lowly colonial. Never mind that he captained a ship and expected immediate acquiescence from his crew when he gave an order. In his case, lives often depended upon immediate compliance.

Was Keyworth one of those Englishmen who still thought Americans traitors to the Crown? That might account for a degree of the hostility the earl hurled Jason's way. There wasn't any other logical reason. Well, other than he'd caught Jason holding Lenora in his arms.

For half a dozen heartbeats, Jason considered defying Keyworth, but calm reason prevailed.

What would it gain to poke the lion?

Particularly if Jason had any intention of pursuing the winsome minx upstairs. *Did* he have intentions? An hour ago, he would've denied such a suggestion and dismissed it as ludicrous.

That was before he'd gazed into unfathomable turquoise eyes.

He'd vow the earl was on the brink of calling him out for nothing more than carrying his injured sister to her bedchamber. Considering they were in full view of several people the whole while, and nothing remotely untoward could occur with so many witnesses, Keyworth's reaction was just shy of melodramatic.

Or addled.

In point of fact, Lenora's brother ought to be thanking Jason for the care he'd taken with his sister.

Regardless, he'd very much enjoyed holding that fragrant bundle of femininity in his arms. Lenora smelled of honeysuckle and orange blossoms. When she'd winked at him, the fetching little firebrand had revealed she wasn't nearly as proper as her older, bearish brother believed.

Would Jason have reacted the same way if he'd found his sister in a stranger's arms?

He considered Keyworth.

Not precisely a stranger, but certainly not an acquaintance or close associate. As he only had younger brothers, Jason couldn't put himself in Keyworth's place. He did know, however, he'd defend his own brothers to the death.

The earl stared stonily at him, the tick in his jaw evergrowing evidence of his rapidly waning patience. Keyworth's reputation as a level-headed, judicious fellow certainly didn't fit the agitated man prowling back and forth behind his desk at the moment.

An eyebrow arched sardonically, Jason complied as he sank into the chair and took the other man's measure. Of similar height, Jason weighed at least a stone more. Perhaps two stone. The earl was likely a deft hand at swords, but Jason was confident he'd fare well if put to the test. In truth, more than one pirate could attest to that fact.

A round in the ring might prove different, however. Jason had no doubt who would come out better in such a match. He could thank his father for his large bones and muscular build. Both characteristics made him an anomaly amongst London's elites, where dandies were known to pad their clothing to give an appearance of a more manly figure.

The earl also took a seat. It didn't escape Jason that the man had positioned himself as the interrogator.

Jason wasn't intimidated. He slung an ankle over his knee and waited.

"Now, tell me exactly what transpired," Keyworth said, his perusal bold and unflinching. He took in Jason's attire, from his missing neckcloth to his dusty boots. "How did my sister acquire her injury, and how did she come to be in your... company?"

Couldn't bring himself to say in Jason's arms, could he?

Jason quirked his mouth into a smug half-smile, unsure whether he admired Keyworth's fierce protectiveness or whether it annoyed the hell out of him.

Regardless, once he'd explained how Lenora had sustained her injury by rushing to his grandmother's aide, Keyworth visibly relaxed.

"Then I thank you for aiding Lenora," he said with good grace.

Their discussion went decidedly south thereafter. Faster than hailstones pummeling the earth during a thunderstorm, in truth.

"I'd like to call upon your sister, Keyworth."

The words were out of Jason's mouth before he'd even mulled them over. Yet, it seemed the most natural thing in the world to want to become better acquainted with the remarkable, courageous, and resourceful woman.

Thoughts of his pending voyage seemed to have slipped their moors too. He could ponder that situation later. He still had time to make a decision and to inform Lady Sethwick and Ronan Brockman.

"No."

One final, inflexible syllable.

Jason's gaze clashed with Keyworth's.

"Might I ask why?" Jason couldn't help but probe.

It wasn't that he wanted to goad Keyworth. Nevertheless, he was genuinely interested in what conclusions Keyworth could've drawn in under fifteen minutes of knowing him.

In point of fact, off the top of his head, Jason could recite several reasons the earl might object to his courting Lenora. The first and foremost was that Jason was an American. He also didn't hold a title, nor was he nobility.

What was more, his wealth would likely seem inconsequential to someone as affluent as Keyworth. Unlike the earl, Jason had earned every penny himself.

From across his desk, his fingers steepled, Keyworth regarded him contemplatively for so long that Jason thought he'd refuse to answer. The recurring *tick-tocking* of the burr walnut drumhead mantel clock, the crackling and occasional hissing of the fire, and a sporadic snore from the enormous Newfoundland sleeping soundly before the hearth filled the tense silence.

At last, Keyworth slumped back into his chair and rested his hands atop the arms. "I only located my sister two years ago, Steele. I'll be tarred and feathered if I permit you or any other man to drag her across an ocean where I might only see her every decade or so."

Two years?

For certain, Jason would like to know that tale in its entirety. Instead of asking the intrusive questions on the tip of his tongue, he chose discretion.

"I'd not heard you'd only recently reunited with your sister," Jason said.

As he'd only met his grandmother a year and a half ago, Jason understood the earl's reluctance.

Keyworth arched an imperious brow. "It's not my story to tell, but suffice it to say, I'm not quite ready to see Lenora married off just yet. So I'll tell you what I've told every other unworthy scalawag who's come sniffing around her skirts. Look elsewhere."

Leaning back in his stuffed armchair, Jason planted his other foot on the floor. "The lady has no choice in the matter?"

What did Lenora think about that?

Did she know?

"You intend to choose her husband?" Jason asked, refusing to examine why the idea infuriated him.

Keyworth's eyes narrowed, and he grew dangerously still.

"Don't be a damned impertinent..." Shaking his head, he sucked in a lengthy breath, then scraped his hand through his hair. "Forgive me. That was beyond the pale. Suffice it to say, Steele, when my sister finds a man she loves and who is willing to sacrifice everything for her, I'll gladly give my blessing to a union. *You* are *not* that man."

Union? Good God.

Jason had met Lenora but a mere two hours ago. Keyworth was putting the cart before the horse. Miles and miles and *miles* before the horse.

How many other would-be-suitors had found the door slammed in their faces before they'd even had a chance to declare themselves to Lenora?

Jason kicked his mouth up on one side and tapped his knee with his fingertips.

"You misunderstand. I'm not proposing, Keyworth."

How had this conversation turned from a wish to know Lenora better to clarifying that Jason wasn't offering marriage? And why did he feel a peculiar disappointment that he couldn't?

"Good," Keyworth returned bluntly, his countenance flat.

The outright rejection shouldn't have stung, but it did.

"I'd never agree to a match between you."

That was crystal clear.

Head canted, Keyworth studied his fingertips before meeting Jason's gaze once more. "Not only because I want Lenora nearby, but because she's not the stuff of which a sea captain's wife is made. She loves too deeply and thrives when surrounded by those she adores. Your long absences would chip away at her. I honestly fear she'd become lonely and likely plagued by the blue devils. Eventually, bitterness and resentment would overtake her."

A scowl pulled Jason's brows together. He couldn't contrive a satisfactory argument against any of those allegations or revelations. It rankled like the devil to have another verbalize his own thoughts. And to be so decisively dismissed as unacceptable, unworthy, and unsuitable, truth be told.

He wouldn't make a bad husband. Perhaps not ideal, but not...*bad*. He'd be faithful, and his wife wouldn't want for anything—except his company.

Bollocks.

How, by all that was sacred, had Jason's musings turned toward qualities that would make him a good husband? Earlier today, he'd been considering how fortunate he was to be carefree and unshackled.

He leveled Keyworth a contemplative glance.

It was *his* fault, blast him.

He'd broached the subject. Planted the seed, and the deuced thing had germinated and taken root in an astonishingly short amount of time. Jason had never liked losing, and being told he was an unfit candidate before he'd even had an opportunity to test Lenora's interest chafed his pride raw.

Keyworth flicked long fingers offhandedly toward Jason. "You have a reputation for being a stellar sea captain. Regardless, if I may be blunt, you are also a rogue. Either, or perhaps both, would destroy Lenora."

Jason scratched his cheek, disliking the grudging admiration Keyworth roused. "I think your sister is much stronger and more resilient than you give her credit."

"Lenora is a great many things admirable," Keyworth agreed, giving the timepiece atop the mantel a swift glance. "I should like to check on her now."

He rose, indicating their meeting was at an end.

Again, the image of her charging the thieves skipped across Jason's mind, and pride rippled across his shoulders. If ever a woman might anchor him to the shore, it would've been a woman like Lenora Audsley.

Alas, it wasn't meant to be.

Jason had a voyage to consider and a grandmother to console. An entanglement at this time wasn't convenient. Keyworth had done him a favor by refusing to permit him to call upon Lenora.

"I shall respect your decision." Summoning a grin, he offered the earl his hand.

Keyworth hesitated and then gripped Jason's palm. "See that you do."

Jason didn't imagine the menace in those four words.

"I'm considering an extended voyage to India soon, in any event." Except the idea held far less appeal than it had a few short hours ago.

Keyworth made a disdainful noise in his throat. "Precisely why you would never suit. If you broke Lenora's heart, I'd have to kill you."

EIGHT

Keyworth House drawing room
Four days later
Late afternoon

Lenora fashioned a polite smile as Lord Phillips, seated to her right on the sofa, continued to babble with Mr. Pew on her left about the intricacies of knotting a cravat. As if either man actually tied their own neckcloths. Delicate china teacup in hand, she glanced around the crowded drawing room, desperate to escape their boring, eye-crossing drivel.

Celestia had recently redecorated the room in shades of blue and white. The effect was quite tasteful and elegant. And yet, the drawing room was welcoming and warm.

The gentlemen's argument had started when Lord Phillips had inquired if a neckcloth had truly been used as a bandage for Lenora's head after the altercation at Burlington Arcade. From there, the discussion digressed to the proper folds and the precise amount of starch required for the most coveted of cravats.

The two gentlemen did *not* agree.

"The waterfall has the most graceful lines," Lord Phillips insisted arrogantly.

"Never say so," objected Mr. Pew with such affront that Lord Phillips might've suggested he wore last Season's fashion. "The cloth must frame a gentleman's neck as does the mathematical cravat."

He pointed confidently to his neckcloth, which was so stiff and high that he could scarcely turn his head.

And men proclaimed women could prattle on about absurd balderdash.

Lenora mentally thanked Captain Steele for not wearing such a fashion travesty, else the other day, she'd have looked as if her head were about to set sail.

"What say you, Miss Audsley?" Mr. Pew put to her.

What?

Having tuned out their squabble, Lenora stared at him blankly.

"You'll have to forgive me, Mr. Pew. I have no knowledge of such things," she improvised. "Therefore, I couldn't possibly make an informed opinion."

Giving a superior sniff, he disdainfully eyed the simple folds of Allen Wimpleton's neckcloth as he stood beside the fireplace in deep discussion with the Marquis of Sterling.

"Just so. Just so," Mr. Pew murmured before he and Lord Phillips resumed bickering like an old married couple, leaving Lenora to woolgather once more.

Landry had refused to consider allowing Lenora to leave her chamber for three days after knocking her head. She'd been perfectly fine the following day except for a walnut-sized lump and a small two-inch cut on her scalp. Never one to enjoy idleness, she'd been bored to distraction thereafter.

This morning, Celestia had mentioned they were to have a *few* more guests for tea than typical. This was not a few. If less than fifty persons were present, Lenora would eat all of the cucumber and salmon sandwiches Cook had prepared.

Lenora detested cucumbers. And salmon.

According to Mama and Celestia, word of Lenora's valiant actions had zipped about the upper salons faster than the great 1666 fire had destroyed much of London. She'd been deemed a heroine. Dozens of bouquets with cards attached, all wishing her a speedy recovery, had arrived over the past days and were currently displayed in the drawing room, dining room, music room, and Lenora's bedchamber.

None had been from Captain Jason Steele.

Lenora resolutely refused to pine after him—a stranger, no less.

He didn't feel like a stranger when he held you against his chest.

Lips firmed, Lenora turned her ponderings in a new direction. Lady Darlington-Pope had sent a lovely silk shawl, a stunning needlepoint reticule to replace the one the thieves had taken, two books, a golden box of fruit-shaped marzipan, a half a dozen gossip rags to read while Lenora convalesced, and a lengthy thank-you note written in swirling script.

Her ladyship had also promised to call as soon as Lenora was recovered while declaring herself *fit as a fiddle* but as bruised as an apple shaken in a barrel.

Whatever that meant.

Each time a new bouquet, a box of chocolates, or some other token arrived, Lenora's heart had sped up, only to have disappointment pool around her toes when she read the accompanying card and it wasn't from Jason.

Stupid, foolish nincompoop.

What had she expected?

In point of fact, she wasn't certain.

Captain Steele had been so kind and considerate—except

for those moments she'd wanted to pinch him for being high-handed. The truth was, she wanted to see him again—still hoped to see him again.

All Landry would say about his discussion with Jason that afternoon he'd seen her home was that he'd thanked the captain for his assistance and that he believed Captain Steele was to take an extended voyage soon.

How soon? To where? How long, precisely, was extended?

None of that was her business.

Lenora's stomach tightened at the idea she might never see Jason again. When she'd first opened her eyelids while lying on the pavement and looked into his mesmerizing gaze, she felt as if she recognized him. As if her soul or spirit did.

It made no sense. It was silly and ridiculous and nonsensical. Lenora and Jason's meeting was happenstance. A coincidence dictated by unfortunate circumstances.

Taking a sip of her tea, Lenora perused the drawing room. She only knew half of those here. The result of her indecorous public display was that an unusually large number of guests had joined the Keyworths for tea today.

Four more curiosity seekers had arrived within the last fifteen minutes.

Poor Mrs. Cox—the cook—and the kitchen maids must be running ragged.

If Lenora wasn't mistaken, the key-shaped brass knocker had echoed a few moments ago, proclaiming another inquisitive member of *le beau monde*. It seemed all of London was touting Lenora as a heroine. Hardly. She had done what any decent person would've done.

She'd wager Lady Darlington-Pope had something to do with all of the hullaballoo and notoriety. Lenora sincerely liked the elderly matron and admired her gumption and perspicacity.

Raising the teacup to her mouth again, she took another sip of the tasty brew and caught the eye of Lady Olivia Wimpleton, who stood near the fireplace speaking to Lady Gambill. Lady Olivia's gaze traveled between Lord Phillips and Mr. Pew, whose conversation had grown so animated that they both gestured wildly.

Lord Phillips nearly poked Lenora in the eye. Only by swiftly leaning backward did she avoid the mishap.

Her blue eyes twinkling, Lady Olivia arched a winged red eyebrow in silent inquiry.

She must've seen the desperation in Lenora's eyes. No rescue would be forthcoming from Landry or Celestia. Their backs were to her as they, the Earl and Countess of Wainthorpe, and Mr. and Mrs. Faulkenhurst, listened intently to something Viscount Kingsley was saying.

Lenora furrowed her brow, trying to remember the connections there. Viscount Kingsley was Lady Olivia Wimpleton's brother, and Ivonne Faulkenhurst was her husband's sister. Of the many members of the *ton* she'd met since coming to London, they were amongst the nicest.

Mama and three of the ladies from her sewing circle were huddled together at a table near the fire. The weather had turned peevish and bitingly cold as October melded into November.

Do you need rescuing? Lady Olivia asked silently across the distance.

Lenora gave an imperceptible nod. *Please.*

Lady Olivia murmured something to Lady Gambill, who smiled broadly—Lady Gambill always presented a rather horsey-toothed smile—and nodded before finding her way to a small cluster of guests. Every now and again, one or two would peer in Lenora's direction before they put their heads together again.

One needn't profess the second sight to know her name was on nearly every tongue.

She disliked being on display.

Lady Olivia made straight for Lenora. "Gentlemen, please do excuse Miss Audsley. I simply must speak to her. It's a matter of some urgency. I'm positive you'll understand."

At once, Mr. Pew and Lord Phillips rose.

After murmuring her excuses, Lenora accepted Lady Olivia's outstretched hand and permitted her to lead her toward the bay window on the other side of the room. The area was only slightly less crowded, and every eye turned in their direction.

Lenora pretended not to notice.

"Those two could bore the bark off of a tree," Lady Olivia said with a broad grin. "What were they discussing so exuberantly? Their latest merino wool tailcoat ordered from Mr. Weston on Bond Street?"

Lenora grinned back. "No. Today's stimulating subject centered around cravats."

Her eyebrows rising, Lady Olivia laughed. Her kind eyes searched Lenora's face. "You are well? I never know how much of the drawing room tattle is accurate. Some are declaring that you throttled two knife-wielding, bear-sized men bare-handed."

Lenora winced inwardly at the image that the description conjured.

"I am fine, Lady Olivia. I suffered a small cut upon my scalp when I fell but was otherwise unhurt."

"I am relieved to hear it." Olivia smiled again. "You look lovely. That mazarine-blue does amazing things to your hair."

"Thank you," Lenora said.

Olivia leaned nearer. "Everyone is always trying to drape us redheads in greens and yellows. I quite like a deep burgundy myself." She smoothed a hand over the front of her rich claret-colored and cream-striped confection.

"And I adore purple and pink." Lenora chuckled. "Mama says peach is acceptable or pale pink, but anything brighter would be gauche with my coloring."

Lady Olivia wrinkled her nose. "A former modiste once insisted I should wear tangerine-orange." She shook her head, her ruby and pearl earrings swinging with the motion. "I detest orange. I refuse to gad about looking like a giant citrus fruit."

Glancing beyond Lady Olivia, Lenora curved her mouth in delight as Merilee Larkins and Lady Diana Marlow, the newest arrivals, made a zigzagging beeline toward her around the other guests. They were a perfumed tempest and a storm in silk and satin. Since their first Seasons out together, they'd become her closest friends.

Turning her attention back to Lady Olivia, Lenora said, "I picked up my ball gown for the Wimpletons' Christmas ball that day of the incident." She gave a wry twist of her mouth. "I confess, it is green and gold."

The gown was a masterful work of art. Ivory satin with shimmering overlays in gold and jade green, the garment was fairy-like. Silver and gold beads, along with hundreds of tiny pearls, gave the material an effervescent glow when the light hit it just so. Her gold silk slippers, also covered in shiny beads and pearls, were nothing short of magical.

"I'm so glad you are attending." Lady Olivia beamed. "My in-laws love nothing better than to host a ball, and I adore dancing. Allen vows I quite wear him out and that he'll have to limit our dances."

The Viscount and Viscountess Wimpleton were famous for their opulent balls and galas, and Lenora doubted Allen

Wimpleton would ever deny his lady anything. They were obviously very much in love.

"I cannot wait to see your gown, Lenora. Is it one of Mademoiselle De la Cour's?" Lady Olivia asked. "She's creating quite a reputation for herself. I commissioned three gowns from her just last week." She winked conspiratorially. "Not a one in any shade of orange."

"It is indeed, though I'm fairly certain Mademoiselle De la Cour is no more French than that covered vase just there." Lenora wiggled her fingers toward a side table where a striking royal blue and gilt ironstone vase overflowed with pink and white roses reposed.

"Lenora." Wearing a cat-in-the-cream grin, Merilee expertly dodged Viscount Corkran's less than subtle attempt to waylay her. The poor man was hopelessly besotted, but as he was a good five inches shorter than Merilee's five feet ten inches, she had deemed him unsuitable.

Lenora felt rather sorry for him. However, the single time Merilee had agreed to a dance, they'd been the object of more than one unkind joke.

The four pretty young ladies hovering around the handsome viscount glowered at Merilee but pasted brilliant smiles upon their faces when the disappointed lord returned his attention to them. Lord Corkran might be short in stature, but his amiable nature, romantic prose, and flair for flattery made him popular with the debutantes. Not to mention his substantial fortune.

Merilee and Diana fashioned polite smiles for Lady Olivia, even though Lenora could see the impatience in their eyes. They were dying to know every last detail of the blundered burglary.

Lenora felt an odd reluctance to share anything about Captain Steele, which was most irregular. She wasn't the possessive sort, especially regarding a man who was scarcely more than a stranger.

Lady Olivia patted Lenora's arm. "My husband is requesting my presence. Please excuse me."

"Thank you, Lady Olivia," Lenora said with heartfelt appreciation.

"We women must stick together." She gave Lenora a brilliant smile and a little wave of her fingers before gliding away.

"Lenora, I tell you, it was all I could do not to storm your bedchamber when I heard of your daring," Merilee gushed as she bussed Lenora's cheek and hugged her. "Was it terribly exciting?"

After doing the same, Diana arched a wry blonde eyebrow. "She thought nothing of invading *my* bedchamber at the ungodly hour of nine the morning after," she said drolly. Her bluebell eyes grew shadowed. "You must've been so frightened, Lenora."

There hadn't been time to be frightened.

Lenora shook her head. "I—"

"She was a veritable Zenobia," a man interjected. "An unflinching, courageous warrior."

Captain Jason Steele.

He's here. He's here, Lenora's heart chanted.

As one, the three women turned.

"Captain Steele." Lenora sounded almost normal. "I didn't know you were expected."

Had he been expected?

Her eyes wide, Merilee breathed, "Oh my."

She did not sound the least normal.

Nudging her in the ribs, Diana said, "Close your mouth before a fly lands inside."

As there weren't any flies in the drawing room, that wasn't likely.

With a disgruntled scowl toward her friend, Merilee snapped her mouth shut. "*He's* the man who carried you to the coach?" She winked at Lenora. "Lucky, lucky girl."

Diana had a somewhat dazed glint in her eyes too, and cool and composed Diana was never awestruck. She personified comportment and equanimity. She sent Lenora a side-eyed glance, then raised an eyebrow archly as if to say, "We shall discuss this—*him*—later."

Lenora firmly told the flush trying to scoot up her neck and face to stay hidden beneath her gown. She wasn't a blushing ninny. She positively had nothing to color about.

Jason bowed, and a lock of his dark hair drifted over his forehead. She liked that he didn't fuss with pomades. A pinkish scar disappeared into his hairline, and a hint of bronze glinted in the sable strands. A testament to his time at sea, no doubt. A waft of soap and bayberry carried to her.

Clean and simple.

Lenora disliked heavily scented gentlemen, particularly those who wore copious quantities of *eau de cologne* or *eau de toilette* to disguise their aversion to bathing. At once, Lord Barnabus Pinwickerly barged to mind. An involuntary shudder skittered from her waist to her shoulders. Lord Pinwickerly was not present today, nor was he usually included in the same circles Landry and Celestia frequented.

Praise God for small favors.

"Miss Audsley," Jason flashed her a smile that was designed to unhinge her knees.

Lenora locked the traitorous appendages against any inclination to turn to custard.

"You look very well," he murmured, still smiling that blinding smile.

She refused to blink rapidly against his masculine onslaught.

Nearby, Lenora heard two distinct sighs of pleasure.

Ninnyhammers and peagooses.

Or was it pea geese?

"I am pleased you've recovered so swiftly." His American accent drew the words out into a deep melodic burr.

"Captain Steele, permit me to introduce my dearest friends." In short order, Lenora had performed the niceties.

The four ladies who'd all but been drooling over Viscount Corkran giggled and then promptly deserted the poor man in favor of joining Lenora and her friends. And Captain Steele, of course.

If they believed she would force Jason to endure their twittering and fawning by performing more introductions, they'd indulged in something much more robust than tea this afternoon.

Good-natured as always, Viscount Corkran gave Jason a curious glance before shrugging a shoulder and joining another group composed of older gentlemen. Not, however, before he'd sent a soulful glance toward Merilee, who was too busy ogling Jason to notice.

Somewhat peevishly, Lenora realized several other ladies also drifted their way. It seemed Jason drew women to his side, as unavoidable as fog descending upon the Thames or rain in November. Except the thick pewter-colored clouds blanketing the sky looked suspiciously like they portended snow.

Wouldn't that be something?

Lenora adored snow. Skating, sleigh rides, making snow angels. Not to mention hot toddies, roasted chestnuts, and steaming cinnamon buns. Mama vowed God had created cinnamon to warm the human heart.

Lenora returned her attention to Jason as the other eager women sidled nearer. A wave of disappointment washed over her, and she dropped her gaze to the carpet for a second lest anyone question her sudden solemnness.

Jason was one of *those* men. Charmers who effortlessly beguiled women. A rogue that attracted the opposite sex like molasses did ants or a candle did a hapless moth—the type of man who caused even sensible women such as Merilee and Diana to blush and become tongue-tied.

He probably had a beautiful woman waiting for him in every port.

Jason noticed the growing cluster of femininity as well, and a flicker of annoyance crossed his face, then it was gone in the next blink.

"Ladies, please forgive me for absconding with Miss Audsley, but my grandmother has specifically requested I locate her rescuer. She wishes to express her appreciation for Miss Audsley's valor."

Valor?

Not a bit of it.

Basic human decency.

Lenora perused the drawing room but saw no sign of the Dowager Countess of Darlington-Pope. Nor Landry or Celestia, for that matter. Perhaps they'd gone to the other salon. So many guests had called this afternoon that Celestia had ordered Teeven to prepare tea in both.

Without awaiting a response, Jason took Lenora by the elbow and neatly guided her toward the entrance. Several gazes followed their progress, and expressions ranged from piqued to inquisitive. She tried to ignore how his large hand engulfed her arm or the pleasurable heat that permeated his glove and warmed her flesh. She failed completely.

Once they were out the door, Jason looked both ways, a furrow creasing his forehead. Instead of leading her toward the salon as she expected, he pulled her into an alcove beneath the curving staircase.

"Whatever are you about, Captain Steele?" Lenora peered behind him, grateful no one had noticed his antics. They only had a minute or two before a servant or a guest passed by, however.

Jason smiled down at her, his expression enigmatic. He lifted her fingers to his mouth and brushed a kiss across her gloved knuckles.

A tingle began at her hand and traveled up her forearm, past her elbow and shoulder, before spreading across her back.

"I'm not supposed to be here today," he murmured against her fingers.

Coming to her senses, Lenora withdrew her hand, albeit reluctantly.

"Why?" She stared up at him, puzzling her forehead.

"I'm not exactly welcome at Keyworth House, Lenora."

NINE

Gazing down into Lenora's upturned face, her brilliant blue-green eyes alive with intelligence and bewilderment, Jason couldn't resist stepping nearer. This was foolhardy, given Keyworth's warning. He shouldn't have come at all, but when Grandmother had requested that he escort her, he'd seized the opportunity.

"You are exquisite today, Lenora. That shade suits you."

The merest hint of color fused Lenora's high cheeks, a contrast to their porcelain smoothness. She slid a glance toward the drawing room, then bit her lip. Several shades darker than her gingery-bronze hair, gold tips accented her thick eyelashes.

Desire throttled through Jason, so powerful it stunned him. He didn't lust after virgins. He had strict standards, and seducing innocents topped the list of prohibited activities. Particularly those who had influential relatives who could easily have him hogtied and stowed aboard a ship sailing to Australia or Timbuktu.

"Why aren't you welcome?" Lenora persisted, her gaze far too perceptive.

He liked that about her—her mettle and cheekiness. She was no faint-hearted miss hiding behind immaculate manners and constrained by Society's strictures. Neither was she a flibbertigibbet or rattlepate.

Brushing his curved finger down her jawline, Jason gave her a closed-mouth smile. How he wished his hands were bare and he could touch what looked to be velvety smooth, ivory skin.

"I asked your brother if I might call upon you."

Her eyes flew wide, and her Cupid's bow, berry red mouth formed an "o" of incredulity.

"You did?"

Was that anticipation or perhaps excitement making her voice slightly breathless?

Jason gave a stiff nod. "I did, but Keyworth said no. Unequivocally. That is also why you didn't receive any flowers from me. I thought it best not to prick the lion, as it were."

Her winged auburn eyebrows drew together over the bridge of her pert nose. A saucy, adorable nose sprinkled with cinnamon-colored freckles.

Did those tantalizing spots cover other places on her body?

None were visible above her modest neckline.

He'd like to press his lips to each and every one as he counted the sun kisses.

Jason didn't deceive himself into believing his only motivation for coming today when he'd been expressly asked not to was to protect Grandmother.

True, that was partially his reason.

Mostly, however, he wanted an opportunity to see Lenora again. He'd been unable to get her out of his mind, her orange blossom-honeysuckle scent from his nostrils, or forget the feeling of her softly rounded body cradled in his arms and pressed to his chest.

Perhaps Jason was beef-witted, but he'd gambled that Keyworth would be away from home this afternoon meeting with his stodgy constituents about Parliamentary matters. On the other hand, if the earl was present, he held a small hope that Keyworth would understand Jason's reluctance to permit Lady Darlington-Pope to venture out and about alone just yet.

"He might've asked me." Lenora pressed her lush strawberry-painted mouth into a stern line. She flicked a glance up at him from beneath lush lashes, partly coy but also partially sincere. "Unless, Captain Steele, there's something about you that he knows, which I do not."

Jason grinned and stepped nearer still—until his trousers brushed the hem of her gown.

If ever there was an unspoken invitation to tell her about himself, this was it. Lenora regarded him with that startlingly clear and unpretentious turquoise gaze. A rarity for women in England but also remarkable for American women.

He liked that about her too. If the truth were known, there was a great deal he esteemed about Lenora Audsley.

Jason dashed a swift glance down the corridor. Luck had been on their side thus far, but with the number of servants and guests circulating this floor, it was only a matter of time before someone came along.

"As much as I would sincerely like to tell you about myself, I fear this may not be the most opportune time. I'd rather your brother not find us here."

He glanced overhead at the ornate curved staircase above their heads.

Lenora followed his gaze and nodded, causing the artfully arranged curls framing her oval face to sway.

"True. Landry is most protective. I shall speak to him." She slid her hand into the curve of Jason's elbow. "I enjoy a brisk walk in Hyde Park every morning at half of eight."

"Indeed." The little minx was providing Jason an opportunity for a rendezvous that wouldn't send Keyworth into apoplexy.

Lenora wasn't a timid mouse but rather chose discretion over confrontation.

She cut him a mischievous glance, the merest hint of a smile playing about the edges of her soft lips. "I know it's not fashionable amongst the *ton*, but mornings are my favorite time of day."

"Half of eight, you say?" Jason curved his mouth into an unabashed, sideways smile.

She nodded again. "Indeed. My maid accompanies me because Mama doesn't rise early. I feed bread crumbs to the ducks swimming in the Serpentine. On occasion, an impish squirrel or a magpie will demand a piece too."

Jason chuckled as he led her down the corridor toward the voices drifting from the salon. "The crust is my favorite part, and cooks everywhere are forever cutting them from my bread."

Lenora giggled, turning her face upward to meet his gaze. "I like the crust too. Mrs. Cox always saves me an end piece for breakfast. Toasted with marmalade."

"I've never tasted marmalade."

"It's scrumptious." She closed her eyes and made a soft, humming noise. "Mmm."

Jason's groin tightened at the sensual image and sound. A sudden desire to see her laid out upon his bed, that glorious hair fanned out across his pillows, his rich port-colored counterpane a backdrop for her ivory body...

Lenora had no idea what she did to him.

He cleared his throat and steered his musings in a safer, less lustful direction. The last thing he needed was a raging cockstand when he encountered his host.

"I'll see if I can charm my cook into giving me a few scraps too." This was a first. Plotting to feed ducks so that Jason might enjoy the pleasure of Lenora's company.

"Should I accompany you inside?" He angled his chin toward the open doorway. "I don't wish for you to suffer your brother's wrath."

"Oh, Landry's not that sort." Lenora squeezed his arm. "He's protective, yes, but he won't begrudge you bringing your grandmother today."

"She has been most determined to see you." He chuckled. "You've become quite a heroine to her. She told me she hasn't experienced this much excitement in decades."

As they entered the salon, Jason was very conscious of the slight lull in the conversations and the many inquisitive gazes turned to regard them. Including Keyworth's. In a room thronging with people, of course, he'd be one of the first to notice Jason and Lenora's entrance.

An expression very similar to a thundercloud descended upon his features, but before he could stomp his way across the thick Aubusson carpet, Grandmother waved Jason and Lenora over.

Keyworth would not make a public scene. He was too controlled and polite to do so, and he wouldn't humiliate Lenora. Nonetheless, he leveled Jason an ominous glare.

Jason grinned, and it became a silent challenge between two dominant males.

Keyworth's wife tugged on his arm and, standing on her toes, said something into his ear.

At once, his countenance cleared, and he bestowed a tender smile upon her. He placed a palm on her tummy and kissed her cheek in full view of all.

Now, *that* Jason approved of.

Keyworth wasn't afraid to show his wife affection like most stuffy Brits were.

With a regal tilt of her head in Jason's direction, Lady Keyworth angled her husband toward a group on the opposite side of the room.

Was the countess subtly aiding Jason?

He distinctly heard the words snow and winter carnival drift from amid the cluster of people. It had looked like snow when he'd helped Grandmother from the coach earlier.

Lady Keyworth was a perceptive woman. And one who knew how to handle her husband, although the earl didn't appear worse for wear for having ceded to his beautiful wife.

Did marriage do that to a man?

Turn him into a spineless wretch? A malleable puppet?

No, but love did. Standing above most men at six inches over six feet, Jason's own father became as docile as a puppy when it came to pleasing his wife.

The thought soured Jason's jovial mood. Why must either the wife or the husband be subjugated? Perhaps it was a concession married people gladly made to keep their spouses content.

"There you are, my dear Miss Audsley. Come. Come. Let me have a look at you." Grandmother held out both of her hands and wiggled her fingers in a summons. "I pray you are no worse for wear for having sacrificed yourself on my behalf."

That brought a chorus of subdued murmurs, and a becoming flush flared over Lenora's cheeks.

"I'm not a hero," she whispered fiercely to Jason. "I wish everyone would stop making a to-do about it. I dislike the attention."

It took but a minute to make their way to his grand-mother. She patted the seat beside her, which another woman had kindly vacated. "Sit beside an old woman and indulge her, won't you, dear?"

With a polite nod, Lenora settled beside Grandmother. As there were no more vacant chairs, Jason stationed himself beside the maroon and gold divan, one hand resting on the carved rosewood back.

Her merry walnut-brown eyes shining, Grandmother took Lenora's hand. "I knew there was something special about you the instant I laid my eyes upon you."

Lenora cast a short glance in Jason's direction before smiling at the elderly woman.

"Thank you, my lady. I only did what anyone would have done."

"Pshaw." Grandmother waved her hand in the air. "We all saw how those cork brains behaved. Cowards, every last one."

It was the truth.

"I don't see any of them here today," Grandmother said. "They're probably afraid my grandson would out their spinelessness." She leaned in, speaking earnestly. "Miss Audsley, I haven't a doubt I would have sustained a serious injury or worse if it hadn't been for your bravery."

"My lady," a stout woman in a gown of an indeterminable and uncomplimentary shade of brown interjected in haughty disbelief. She pressed a hand to her substantial bosom theatrically. "Are you implying Miss Audsley saved your life while others stood by and did nothing at all?"

"Indeed, Lady Clutterbuck. That is precisely what happened. Miss Audsley held those two ruffians off until my grandson arrived."

Grandmother bestowed a doting smile upon Jason.

He still hadn't told her of his possible voyage to India. A journey that didn't seem half as enticing as it had mere days ago. His attention shifted to Lenora's slightly bowed neck topped by vibrant red curls.

She hates this.

Lenora truly detested all of the attention.

"Grandmother, you asked me to remind you to invite Miss Audsley, her mother, and the Earl and Countess of Keyworth to supper Saturday as a way to express your appreciation."

Jason gave her a lopsided boyish smile, praying she wouldn't expose his taradiddle.

Blinking owlishly for a moment, his grandmother's sharp gaze drifted to Lenora before she jerked it back to him. He knew the instant she understood. Approval shone in her eyes.

"I had forgotten. I've been too busy retelling the story of Miss Audsley's heroic actions." She chuckled and shook her head, giving Lenora a fond smile. "The cat's out of the bag now, however. Do say you'll honor an old woman's dearest wish, Miss Audsley, and join me for dinner Saturday."

Grandmother speared Jason a telling glance, and he felt sure he'd be explaining himself on the way home. Only, he didn't have an explanation.

"I should like that very much, my lady," Lenora said without waiting for her brother's approval. She had a backbone and an independent streak too.

By that time, Lord and Lady Keyworth had neared. From the deep lines riveting Keyworth's forehead, he'd heard the exchange and was not pleased. He couldn't very well refuse to accept, or else he'd appear churlish. After all, no one but he and Jason knew the precise nature of their conversation in the study the other day.

Keyworth hadn't breathed a word about Lenora staying away from *Jason.* Only the reverse. He couldn't entirely prevent the pleased twitch of his lips but wasn't lackbrained enough to permit a full-on smile.

The earl could only be pushed so far.

"Dinner would be lovely," Celestia chimed in, looping her hand through Keyworth's arm and hugging it to her side. "I believe you possess an extensive collection of antique writing utensils, Lady Darlington-Pope. As a scrivener, I'll admit to a deep curiosity about them."

If memory served him correctly, Jason believed Ronan Brockman had mentioned that Lady Keyworth's father and uncle were scribes and her ladyship was an accomplished amanuensis herself.

"I do indeed, Lady Keyworth." Grandfather had permitted her that one minor entertainment. "I even possess an Egyptian reed pen and a Roman stylus. I would be honored to show them to you Saturday."

"I very much look forward to it," the countess said, placing a hand on her stomach.

Mrs. Smith bustled into the room, her face flushed. Though whether from pleasure or tension, Jason couldn't be sure. The moment she spied Lenora, she made directly for her.

"I wondered where you'd disappeared to," she said. "Lady Diana and Miss Larkins said they'd last seen you leaving the drawing room with Captain Steele."

The quintessence of ladylike serenity, Lenora smiled up at her mother. "Indeed, Mama. Lady Darlington-Pope wished to speak with me."

So had Jason, but she'd omitted that particular.

"Of course, she did," Mrs. Smith acknowledged with maternal pride. "Reporters for *The Courier*, *The London Chronicle*, and *The Star* have left their cards. They wish to interview you." Her gaze gravitated to Grandmother. "Likely you as well, my lady."

"I have no interest in speaking to those truth twisters," Grandmother scoffed. "Reporters rarely report the facts.

Omissions and calculated slants are more up their nefarious, self-serving alleys. Unless, of course, they can cause a bit of ruination by printing rumors and *on dit*."

Grandmother was not a fan of newspapers or gossip sheets, as she called them.

"I'd prefer you didn't either, Lenora." Keyworth rubbed beneath his eye with a bent knuckle. "The attention mightn't all be complimentary."

"La, it's far too late for that," Lady Clutterbuck trilled, fluttering her hands.

So absorbed in Lenora, Jason had all but forgotten the woman sitting across from her and his grandmother.

"There was an article printed in *The Morning Post* today written by an eyewitness," Lady Clutterbuck gloated.

Likely one of the cowards who'd refused to lend Lenora assistance.

Several people floated nearer, and many who didn't regarded them with keen interest.

Lady Clutterbuck preened under the attention now fixed on her. Eyes bright and mouth prim, she perused her rapt audience. "The accompanying drawing is most..." She crumpled her doughy face as she searched for an appropriate term. "*Unflattering.*"

"How so?" Keyworth asked the two words in a tone as cold and sharp as fresh-cut marble. Evidently, he did not subscribe to *The Morning Post*. It wasn't terribly surprising with a dozen or more other newssheets available.

"*Well...*" Lady Clutterbuck said with the dramatic air of a seasoned actress, "Miss Audsley is shown in a state of *dishabille.*" She shifted her hungry gaze toward Jason, giving him a bold appraisal. "Captain Steele appears to be leering at her nearly exposed bosom."

TEN

Laughing as a particularly greedy duck nipped her half boot, Lenora tossed the last of the bread crumbs to the hungry waterfowl gathered around her feet and paddling in the water near the shore. "Away with you before you bite my toes."

A few feet away but close enough to provide acceptable chaperonage, Dottie, her maid, flirted with a footman. At the same time, his mistress, Mrs. March, enjoyed her daily constitutional and briskly strolled the Serpentine's path.

Few of *le beau monde's* elite roused themselves from their luxurious beds this early in the day, much less to take the air in a park covered with three inches of snow. The exception was Mrs. Ann March, a widow who walked on the opposite shore. She circled the Serpentine precisely three times each morn before climbing into her coach.

There were also two gentlemen on horseback Lenora wasn't acquainted with. As they stayed on Rotten Row,

Lenora only saw them from a distance. Others visited the park, but those three were the only ones to do so at the same time and as often as Lenora.

Therefore, her clandestine encounters with Jason remained their secret.

For now.

Hopefully for the foreseeable future too. Until Lenora could define what was happening between them. Guilt nibbled at her conscience for sneaking behind Landry's back. She hadn't asked him why he'd forbidden Jason to call upon her. She knew his reasons. They were legitimate concerns for a loving brother.

Lenora wasn't sure whether she was reckless or daring for continuing to meet with Jason. Regardless, she did know she wasn't ready to put an end to their time together.

Jason hadn't mentioned his upcoming voyage, and not wanting to put a damper on their budding relationship, she hadn't asked him about the journey. She feared the answer wouldn't be to her liking, and for the present, she wanted to pretend they might actually have a future together.

Her folly might—probably—would lead to heartache later.

It was unlikely, but should Landry learn she'd *bumped* into Jason at Hyde Park a time or two, he would have to chalk it up to chance. After all, if Jason chose to frequent the park the same hour she did, who was she to say he couldn't?

As long as her brother didn't know they'd been meeting for weeks now. Besides, Landry had never told her that she couldn't see Captain Steele.

Lenora had managed an extended walk almost every day since her recovery, and quite coincidentally—or so she insisted to Dottie—Captain Steele had been waiting at the Serpentine several of those days.

From the knowing glint in the maid's eyes, she suspected the truth. But as she was engaged in a serious flirtation with Mrs. March's handsome footman, the lovestruck servant wasn't going to do anything that would curtail their morning excursions.

Specifically, she wouldn't be telling Landry.

If it weren't for these outings, Lenora didn't know when she'd see Jason.

Unfortunately, Lady Darlington-Pope had taken to her bed with a nasty chest cold after inviting them for dinner. Their supper invitation had been postponed indefinitely, for which Lenora thought Landry secretly rejoiced. The much-anticipated Wimpletons' Christmas ball would be upon them in no time.

Would Jason still be here?

Had he received an invitation, and if so, would he attend?

Would he ask Lenora to dance?

She wanted that very much. It would provide another opportunity to be in his arms.

They couldn't keep sneaking around to see each other. Well, Lenora and Jason could, but it was a rather chilly courtship. If one could call it that.

She sent Jason a sidelong glance, too aware of the contours and muscles his greatcoat hid. Would it be wrong to pray and ask God for something so selfish—that Jason stay in England? At least a while longer?

As if sensing her perusal, he turned his head. An emotion she couldn't identify flickered in his eyes.

Lenora ought to be chagrinned at being caught staring, but she wasn't. Somehow, she knew he understood. She'd found him doing the same thing several times and always with a crease between his eyebrows as if he fought an inner battle.

Giving her a boyish grin, he folded the small brown sack

he'd brought his own bread scraps in and tucked it into his triple-capped greatcoat's pocket.

Lenora pointed a finger at her forehead, near the hairline, while staring at the mark upon his at the exact same place. "Is that where you were injured during your scuffle with the pirates?"

At his surprised look, she lifted a shoulder.

"I couldn't help but hear what you told Mama that day I was injured."

"Yes, during a sword fight, I tripped over a rope and cracked my head upon the ship's rail. Nothing so dashing as having tossed a salty buccaneer into the ocean."

"A sword fight?" She swallowed at the image.

"Piracy isn't nearly as rampant as it once was." He winked rakishly. "You needn't fret on my account, sweeting."

He was dangerous when he was deliberately charming, and at this moment, Captain Jason Steele was very dangerous indeed.

Lenora fumbled around for a topic less likely to incinerate her.

"I never thanked you for being so kind to Mama that day or for playing along with my little charade," Lenora said, another wave of appreciation warming her.

Jason regarded her for a long moment before saying simply, "You're welcome."

She'd expected him to pontificate slightly more. But she was learning that Jason never said more than he needed to. A man of few words, he wasn't, but neither did he babble on about nonsensical claptrap such as a neckcloth's folds.

Tilting his head, he squinted at the cloudy sky. "I believe we can expect more snow before nightfall."

"I like the snow," Lenora said, watching as little vapor puffs formed with each word. "It makes everything feel clean and protected. There's a kind of peacefulness when everything is blanketed with snow."

"I like snow too," he said as the snow crunched beneath his glossy Hessians. "We get quite a lot of it in Boston."

Lenora brushed away a smattering of breadcrumbs clinging to her cloak. "In Brighton, there was a winter carnival each year—snow or not. When it snowed, there were sleigh rides, sledding, and ice skating."

She'd never participated but had always longed to. Papa believed such frivolities spoiled the soul, and Mama always feared some manner of harm would befall Lenora.

Though it wasn't visible, she looked toward the River Thames. "I've heard there have been years that the Thames has frozen over and Londoners have celebrated with Frost Fairs. Both are quite rare, however." Her attention drifted back to the man-made lake before them. "Do you suppose they allow skating on the Serpentine if it freezes?"

Jason nodded, his eyes more blue-gray today, likely because of the clouds overhead. "I believe so. Though it's cold, there's little chance of the lake freezing solid enough this early on. It takes many days of freezing weather to create a surface hard and safe enough to stand on."

He caught her gloved hand in his, hers white against his black, and she shot a quick glance at Dottie. She was too busy beguiling her footman to notice Jason's forwardness.

"Do you skate, Lenora?"

They'd taken to addressing each other by their given names when alone. Jason still clasped her hand as if it were the most natural thing in the world. It would have been if they were betrothed or married. As they were neither, holding hands was highly inappropriate.

Regardless, Lenora didn't withdraw her hand.

She shook her head in answer to his question, grateful for

the velvet hood covering her. Her wool, silk feathered redingote didn't provide enough protection from the biting cold.

"No. Mama was afraid I'd get hurt." Mama meant well, but her concern had been suffocating at times. Lenora supposed it was because she couldn't have children of her own, and Lenora was the only child she would ever have.

"Is that why you don't walk Keyworth's dog? He's too big for you to safely control?" At her surprised glance, he quirked a brow. "I've seen him. He must weigh ten stone or more."

"Sampson is gentle and very sweet-tempered. However, he can be a bit much to handle when he's excited." She swept a gaze up and down the path. "In fact, it was near here, just there, that he knocked the Duchess of Westfall down."

She pointed to a section of trees lining the pathway. "She wasn't the duchess then, of course, and Sampson was just a puppy. His Grace, the Duke of Westfall, played the hero that day because Her Grace had sprained her ankle when she fell. They fell in love and married a short time later."

"Sampson is a matchmaker?" he said with an undercurrent she couldn't quite identify but which sent shivers zipping from her waist up her spine. "A very romantic tale indeed."

Lenora curved her mouth into a nascent smile, feeling oddly poignant and sentimental for no reason she could pinpoint. "It is, isn't it?"

Jason released her hand, then took her arm. As always, a jolt of sensual awareness billowed through her. That happened every time they touched. It was a wonder she had any bones left in her at all.

After Lenora nodded to Dottie to indicate she and the captain were going to walk the Serpentine's path as they had in previous days, he said, "You must permit me to teach you to skate."

Lenora's heart quickened at the idea of his arm around her

waist as he held her upright. The thought warmed her from the inside out before another less pleasant one turned her heart cold.

"I don't think that likely, Jason. Landry says you are to sail soon."

His jaw went taut for two paces, but then he crooked an eyebrow. "I haven't decided yet whether to accept the commission. I'm reluctant to leave my grandmother, especially after her bout of ill health. She's all alone except for me."

"It's obvious you care for her very much."

"I do, though I've only known her a short while—not quite a year and a half."

Lenora understood exactly what he meant. She adored Landry and Celestia, and she'd only known them for two years. "I first met Landry two years ago."

"He said as much to me."

When he'd warned Jason away from Lenora?

Was it because Landry couldn't stand the idea of losing her so soon after he'd finally found her?

Jason smiled down into her eyes, and Lenora's stomach flopped over itself. This man was coming to mean too much to her. She was terrified to explore the burgeoning emotion.

A dour thought impaled her contentment.

After his grandmother died, would Jason ever return to England?

What need was there for him to?

Lenora could never live a continent away from her family. How had Mrs. Steele endured the isolation, especially in a new country?

"Besides, a letter arrived from my mother yesterday." Jason skimmed his gaze over the park festooned in white. "For the first time in nearly three decades, she's returning to England to visit her mother. She plans on staying until spring. This will be her first Christmas with her mother since she was twenty years old."

Lenora oughtn't to ask. It wasn't any of her business. And still, her obstinate tongue formed the words. "What kept her away so long?"

Jason's intense gaze probed hers before he broke the connection. Indicating a nearby bench, he urged her toward it. "It's a long tale, I fear." He brushed the snow off the bench. "Have a seat, and I'll try to abbreviate the story."

Lenora sat and didn't object when he sat far too close for propriety's sake. His thigh brushed hers, but it was so cold that she welcomed the heat. In fact, she leaned into his beckoning warmth and murmured, "Tell me what you will."

Jason spoke in low tones for several minutes, and Lenora listened. At times anger or compassion made his voice rise or fall. "I think my mother has been afraid to return, even after her father died. She's been away more years than she lived with her parents, and she and her mother might've become strangers."

Landry had been a stranger to Lenora, but now he was the dearest brother.

"Regardless, I believe my mother now wishes to see her mother before Grandmother leaves this world," Jason said.

"It's such a sad story of stubbornness and unforgiveness." Lenora peeked up at him, liking the lazy smile arcing his mouth. "Nonetheless, I'm glad you sought out your grandmother. She's truly a dear."

He chuckled, the sound rumbling around his broad chest and heating her insides like mulled cider sipped before a blazing hearth. "She's a stubborn old bird but possesses a brilliant wit and a heart big enough to hold the ocean."

"Hmm, she sounds like my mother." Lenora kicked at a pebble atop the snow. "Not my birth mother. I never knew her. But my adopted mother has never made me feel anything less than her own child."

He slipped his arm around her shoulders, drawing Lenora even nearer. She truly ought to protest, but it was so cozy, and it seemed completely fitting.

"How is it you didn't meet your brother until two years ago?"

Lenora breathed out a long, controlled breath, recalling the day an investigator had knocked upon their cottage door and announced she was the sister of an earl. "It is also a sad story but with a happy ending. At least, partially happy."

Lenora told him how Landry's father—an unkind and unforgiving man—had learned that his wife had taken a lover after years of abuse. Lenora was the result of their affair. The old earl killed Lenora's father and then took her from the countess when Lenora was mere hours old. He'd never told his wife where he'd sent the child.

"On her deathbed, my mother told Landry of my existence and begged him to find me. He searched nonstop for eight years."

Her gaze caught Jason's, and she didn't blush because of the moisture pooling in hers.

"Most men would've stopped searching long before that, but not Landry. He would not give up." Emotion made her voice crack. "And not only did he take me in, but Mama too. He's treated her as a cherished relative."

Jason brushed a fingertip at the corner of her eye, wiping away the lone tear that had escaped. "He's a wonderful brother."

Suddenly, he missed his brothers' comradery and good-natured insults and jests.

Fingering the silver cloak clasp at her neck, Lenora grinned. "He truly is."

Jason quirked an eyebrow and skewed his mouth up on one side. "Laureen Smythe-Shufflebottom?"

Giggling, Lenora shook her head. "Afraid of someone learning of my identity, Mama changed my first name. She changed our last name to Smith after my adopted father died. His pregnant mistress pushed him down a flight of stairs when he wouldn't renounce his vocation and leave Mama and me."

She'd never spoken of that ugliness with anyone but Landry. Not even Mama. Somehow, it felt fitting to share such intimate details with Jason.

He took her gloved hand in his and linked their fingers. "I like Laureen, but Lenora fits you better. Probably because that's how I've known you."

"You think so?" She wrinkled her nose. "I've always wanted a sophisticated name like Alexandra or Josephine. Or even something exotic such as Domonique or Antoinette. But then, an illegitimate noblewoman's daughter ought not to have lofty aspirations."

With his other hand, Jason gently turned her face until his eyes bored into Lenora's soul. "Never disparage yourself, Lenora. You are an extraordinary, intelligent, and courageous young woman."

Emotion clogged her throat, and her eyes misted.

Unforeseen and unwarranted anger suddenly gripped her that he could reduce her to a watering pot with such practiced ease. Men of his ilk could always wrap women around their little fingers with a seductive glance or smile.

She lifted her chin, just short of tossing her head. Such overt theatrics were not what she was made of.

"I vow, Jason, you say that to all the women you have waiting for you in various ports around the world." Waving her hand, she continued in a singsong voice. "Remarkable. Unique. Extraordinary. Unparalleled..."

A throaty growl reverberated in his throat, and Lenora stuttered to a stop.

Jason's features had turned to granite, and a flinty hardness that she'd never seen before entered his hazel eyes. His words were clipped and raspy. "*No* women are awaiting me at any port unless you count my mother amongst their numbers."

Chagrin promptly chastised her. What he did was none of her business, and it was beyond the pale for her to judge him. It wasn't her place to try to change him either.

"I'm sorry, Jason. That was not well done of me."

His anger evaporated as swiftly as it had manifested, and a teasing gleam crinkled the corners of his face.

"Why, if I didn't know better, I'd think you were jealous, Lenora."

Now it was her turn to become vexed.

"Jealous?"

Jealous? Preposterous.

Was it?

That unwanted thought further fueled her irritation.

"I am no such thing, you arrogant chucklehead."

"Such unkind words coming from such sweet lips," he murmured.

Her gaze locked with his, and something indescribable within the depths of his eyes touched her spirit. Her tirade flew away like the down of a thistle in a windstorm with her next irregular breath. This man had her at sixes and sevens. Blowing hot and then cold, then hot again, all with a single sizzling look.

She darted her tongue out to moisten her dry lips.

With a gravelly groan, Jason encased her in his strong embrace and captured her mouth. His lips were velvety firm and warm and tasted of mint and tea.

Lenora permitted her lashes to flutter shut. How could she not when something akin to warm honey or melted chocolate had replaced her blood, and every joint seemed to have softened to the consistency of fresh custard?

I'm undone.

ELEVEN

Wimpleton's Christmas Ball
Mayfair, London England
15 December 1820
Half of eleven o'clock

Jason leaned a shoulder against a wall adorned with Chinese silk damask wallpaper. Birds and blossoms covered the wall in shades of pale aqua-blue, peachy pinks, and saffron. The paper was a bit busy for his taste.

He flicked his pocket watch closed after determining the time had come for setting his plan in motion. Acquainted with few of those in attendance, it had been easy to stick to the shadows and corners—to remain unobtrusive and inconspicuous until the moment was right.

In point of fact, that wasn't precisely accurate.

At least a dozen females had boldly assessed him in the manner a horse breeder might eye a possible stud for his broodmares. Females needn't be scantily clad and sauntering the docks or loitering near the countless unsavory pubs and gaming dens to have a harlot's heart beating within their breasts.

The difference was, the unfortunate women prostituting themselves on the streets had little recourse. The perfumed and powdered Society ladies who readily offered up their voluptuous charms did. But because only the former did so for a fee, she was degraded and demeaned.

Jason made a slow sweep of the ballroom with his gaze. The rise and fall of chatter and laughter blended with the orchestra. Elegantly attired women, dripping in jewels and swathed in silk and satin, circled the sanded ballroom floor with regal gentlemen, almost all wearing identical evening black.

Across the room, Grandmother sat busily chatting with her cronies. She pointed her hand-painted, black lace-edged fan toward a portly dandy stuffed into an orange ensemble better suited to forty years ago. He ought to have chosen black like most of the other gentlemen present. All the fellow needed was a towering wig and a heart-shaped *mouche* on his face to appear a complete fopping coxcomb.

Suddenly, the intimate little group erupted into peals of laughter.

Jason didn't want to know what his grandmother had said to send her compatriots into fits of the giggles, but he could well guess.

He'd wager his small fortune the gentleman's unfortunate choice of wardrobe combined with his spindly legs and round torso had him relegated to a citrus fruit—an orange or tangerine, or perhaps a tropical fruit such as a papaya.

Not one of Grandmother's coconspirators was a day under seventy. All appeared to be having a grand time poking fun at several other dandies or ladies who'd made a poor choice in dress this evening.

Jason was acquainted with Allen Wimpleton, his hosts' son, and he hadn't had to press his friend hard to ensure he received an invitation to tonight's ball. It seemed London's holiday season couldn't officially begin until the Wimpletons launched the festivities with their annual Christmastide ball. It was a much-anticipated event amongst *le beau monde.*

The ball heralded the distinction of boasting at least one couple becoming betrothed every year since its inception nearly three decades ago.

He and Grandmother had only been here an hour. She'd insisted on arriving fashionably late—a trend he thought perhaps was more popular thirty years ago than presently. Since setting aside her mourning weeds, Grandmother had attended balls, routs, assemblies, and the like with the eagerness of a first-Season debutante.

Jason had often pondered just how controlling and restrictive his grandfather had been. Grandmother wouldn't discuss him nor anything about her deceased husband. Nonetheless, her features hardened around the edges, and a slightly haunted shadow dimmed the sparkle in her brown-eyed gaze whenever the dead earl was mentioned.

Jason was glad she was determined to live the remainder of her life to the fullest. Just last night at dinner, she'd announced that she was considering whether she might take a tour of the continent.

"I wish to see something of the world before I die, Jason."

Not by herself, by God. And not with only Myrtle as her companion. Maybe his mother would agree to accompany her. She and Father were expected from America any day now.

It took him somewhat by shock to realize how protective he'd become of his grandmother in the last year and a half. He sincerely worried about her and was concerned she was over-doing it since her recent ill-health. She only managed evening activities by taking a several hours long nap beforehand. Tonight, she'd slept until eight, when her maid had awoken her and dressed her for the ball.

A grin edged Jason's mouth up on one side.

She was resplendent in vivid poppy-red and gold tonight. He vowed an entire flock of parrots had given up their plumage for her coiffure. Her evident happiness caused a swell of emotion behind his ribs.

He didn't know much about his grandfather, but if his delightful, big-hearted wife and kind, soft-spoken daughter were happier with the sod removed from their lives, Jason didn't need to know more. The previous Earl of Darlington-Pope had been a tosspot.

Just as Jason had determined to seek out Lenora, a trio of resplendent dames sailed past and spied him lurking near a column. They looked him over from head to toe.

"Isn't *he* that American sea captain?" the rounded lady with prominent front teeth lisped sotto voce.

"Hmm," another with enough bosom exposed a stork might nest in her ample cleavage mused. She trailed her tongue over her lower lip and stared boldly at Jason's groin. "I don't care what country he's from, only how skilled he is with his *sword*," she purred.

He cringed inwardly, put off by her attempt at bold seduction.

"Melinda," the first scolded on a high-pitched titter while swatting her friend on her arm with her fan. "You are so naughty."

She didn't seem nearly as scandalized as titillated. Her too-bright eyes and flushed skin betrayed her.

"As I do not count traitorous colonials amongst *my* acquaintances, *I* would not know," the third, a haughty and skeletally thin lady, sniffed. "It seems the Wimpletons are inviting all manner of riffraff these days. Americans, shop girls, merchants, illegitimate..."

She stuttered to a stop when Jason bent into an exaggerated bow and, elevating an eyebrow, trailed a leisurely gaze over the three.

Assuming a lazy drawl, he murmured, "Don't forget bigoted, bumptious, critical harpies."

As one and so synchronized as to have been practiced, the three sucked in affronted gasps. Presenting their backs, they stalked away, a stream of invectives trailing behind them.

The Wimpletons' butler had also known Jason was an American. Looking down his bulbous nose, the servant had announced Jason and Grandmother in a practiced, monotone drone.

How did one keep *any* inflection from their tenor?

"Adalia Glenister, the Dowager Countess of Darlington-Pope..." The majordomo's superior tone had taken on an arrogant, disapproving air. "And Captain Jason Steele."

Rather than seek Lenora out straightaway and run the risk of her brother's wrath ruining her evening, Jason had bided his time. He'd scarcely been able to tear his attention away from her since arriving.

Her gown was an otherworldly confection of green and gold. Her red hair shone like an evening star, and her alabaster skin looked carved from the finest marble. An ethereal glow radiated from her.

Time and time again, Jason had stopped himself from striding to Lenora, sweeping her into his arms, and carrying her away to claim her as his. Such brashness guaranteed an appointment on the field of honor the next day, even if he married her first. Which would be deuced tricky to do without a special license and her consent.

A coin slipped to a frazzled servant provided Jason with

the information he sought upon arrival—which dances were waltzes and was supper to be served at midnight?

Four of the scheduled dances were indeed waltzes. And yes, supper would be served at midnight directly after the supper dance, which happened most fortunately to be a waltz. Jason intended to be Lenora's partner for both.

He'd asked her to save the supper dance for him when they'd last met at the Serpentine in Hyde Park.

Delight creasing the corners of her eyes, she'd agreed.

"Landry will be vexed," she'd admitted frankly. "Though I don't know why he is so set against you."

"It's because I'm a sea captain." Since they were speaking candidly, he might as well be forthright too. "He doesn't believe I can put down roots."

Her nose red from the cold, Lenora had cocked her head and studied him like a curious bird. A little red-nosed bird. "Can you? Put down roots, that is?"

Jason had been saved from answering when a dog ran past, and a frazzled footman had given chase.

In truth, he hadn't believed he could settle down until a red-headed spitfire had taken on two thieves with no thought to her own safety. Now, however, he was convinced he could. With her. The matter of where they'd live—America or England—was significantly more than a pebble in his shoe.

If he could convince Lenora to be his. And *if* her brother didn't call Jason out.

He frowned as a fawning milksop guided Lenora back to Lady Keyworth's side. Jason didn't miss the way the pup's hand rested low on her delicate back, just above her nicely rounded bottom.

If the swain dared trail his fingers any lower, he'd be nursing a broken hand, by God.

Jason straightened, and after pulling his waistcoat back

into place and adjusting the cuffs of his coat, he wended through the guests with one purpose. To reach Lenora's side and request the supper dance.

Thank goodness Keyworth wasn't still hovering about his wife. He was across the room near the punch bowl. Hopefully, he didn't intend to give his increasing duchess a cup. Jason had seen Mr. Pew empty a full flask into the concoction, not more than a quarter of an hour ago.

As he approached, Lenora glanced up, and a radiant smile lit her beautiful face. Again, his heart squeezed as it was wont to do when she graced him with a smile. Or a glance from beneath her lashes. Or when she laughed.

Lord, he'd never known a woman's laugh could light up a room or send his pulse to singing. Her laughter bubbled forth as a contagious, musical melody, unfettered and joyous.

"Captain Steele. I'd given up hope of seeing you this evening," Lenora said, running her fingers along her fan's delicate handle.

Had she truly?

The twinkle in her turquoise eyes belied her comment. She'd trusted Jason would come, just as he'd known she'd save the supper dance for him.

He bowed to her and Lady Keyworth, cognizant of the rapt female gazes trained on him. American women might be more outspoken and unhesitatingly voice their opinions, but British women undressed men with their eyes. Since arriving in London, Jason could've had a different woman warm his bed every night.

Certainly, he was no monk, but he wasn't a libertine either. Casual sex with a stranger held no appeal.

"My grandmother insisted it was impolite to arrive on time," he murmured, pointedly keeping his focus on the two women before him and not the frenzied whispering a few feet away. "An opinion I do not share."

"I quite agree with you, Captain Steele," Lady Keyworth said. "I cannot abide tardiness, even if it is *de rigor*."

Jason extended his hand. "My dance, I believe, Miss Audsley."

Lenora didn't even glance toward her sister-in-law for affirmation that she might accept his offer. "I did promise you," she said in her guileless, unpretentious way.

"You'd best hurry," her ladyship murmured with a discreet shifting of her gaze behind them by way of a warning. "My husband approaches."

A judicious woman.

At once, Jason clasped Lenora's hand to help her rise. Without sparing a glance behind him, Jason led her in the opposite direction at a pace that might have been brisker than was entirely polite.

"Are we running away from my brother?" Lenora laughed huskily. "He's truly not an ogre, Jason."

"I refuse to let him steal what I've been anticipating for days." Jason skillfully maneuvered them through the crowd toward the dance floor.

"Oh? And what is that?" the little minx asked far too innocently.

"Lenora, keep looking at me like that, and I'll be whisking you into a private alcove to steal a kiss."

TWELVE

A lovely idea indeed, but Lenora wasn't foolhardy enough to try to slip from the ballroom when she had no doubt Landry's focus was firmly riveted on her and Jason. Instead, she smiled and took her place on the dance floor.

"As tempting as your offer is, Jason, I think it best not to rouse my brother's wrath deliberately."

The orchestra began playing, and he skillfully swept her around the room. Lenora kept her gaze trained on the dimple in his chin. At least she tried to. Every now and again, her attention gravitated toward his mouth as she recalled their kiss in Hyde Park.

If she closed her eyes, she could still feel Jason's mouth and taste the mint and tea on his tongue. A frisson sluiced through her at the poignant memory. In truth, she wouldn't mind hieing off to a private niche and further practicing the art of kissing.

But as she'd said to Jason, Landry was sure to follow. While she appreciated his concern, this obsession with keeping Jason at bay had grown tiresome. Lenora was a grown woman, for pity's sake. Soon to be one and twenty, she well knew her own mind.

And Lenora wanted Jason.

She'd admitted that truth to herself after their kiss.

Whether he could be the kind of man she needed was something she couldn't be positive of. Yet. A worry niggled incessantly in the back of her mind. Without his saying so, she knew he could no more permanently leave America than she could leave England. Their families meant too much to both of them.

That dour fact put a damper on her mood but only for one stanza of the waltz. This was now, and she would enjoy the moment. No one knew what tomorrow would bring.

"Lenora?" Jason's voice held a husky note she hadn't heard before.

Desire?

Tilting her head, she met his gaze, and her breath caught. Aye, smoldering desire. For her.

"You shouldn't look at me like that." Her voice was also a throaty rasp. Regardless, she couldn't pull her gaze away to see if anyone else noted his intense regard.

Edging her nearer, he murmured into her ear, "Like what, sweetheart?"

Her heart somersaulted at the endearment. Or mayhap it was the warmth of Jason's breath caressing her ear that sent her pulse into double-time.

"Like you want to devour me."

"Perhaps I do."

She bit her lower lip against the words hovering on the edge of her tongue.

Perhaps I want you to.

But there were no promises between them. Nothing more than a growing attraction to a man from another country who would never stay in England. What was more, Lenora's mother's disgrace was a mantle she could not easily shed. Not because Society held it against her, though a few of the *ton* did.

No, it was more that she couldn't make a colossal mistake as her mother had. She knew from personal experience what happened to illegitimate offspring. Few understood the stigma that always shadowed a person of that station.

As if sensing her confusion, Jason murmured, "Stop thinking so much. Let the music take you away."

And so she did for a few minutes.

Lenora pretended that there might be something lasting and permanent between her and Jason. She let herself believe he felt the same for her and that this foreign feeling that grew daily was love.

Didn't love conquer all?

All too soon, the music faded away, and a note from a violin lingered after the other instruments. Lenora and Jason stopped but didn't immediately step away from each other.

It was sure to garner attention, and still, Lenora was incapable of moving an inch. She was locked in the grasp of something undefinable. Something far more significant than her or Jason and far more commanding than mere willpower.

"Lenora, darling, I..." Looking past her, Jason abruptly stopped. "Damn."

Finally, Lenora summoned the ability to step away from his embrace and glanced over her shoulder.

Landry.

Her brother's forced smile didn't reach his arctic eyes.

Celestia gave Lenora an apologetic glance. Lenora loved her sister-in-law all the more for understanding. Celestia adored her husband, but she was a practical woman with an even temperament. She didn't make assumptions either.

"Do join us for supper, Captain. Lenora." Landry's tone brooked no argument. "I have a table reserved."

It was probably a table situated in a corner where he might take her and Jason to task for their public display.

Tension, weighty and thick, accompanied the foursome to the table draped in pristine white with an evergreen and holly centerpiece that Landry led them to. After everyone had settled into their respective seats, the waiters brought them plates piled high with all manner of delicacies and filled their champagne flutes.

Landry picked up his fork. "I ran into Ronan Brockman and Viscount Sethwick at White's today." He cut an asparagus spear covered in white sauce. "He mentioned your pending voyage to India. You're to sail within the week, Brockman said. A journey of some months, perhaps as much as a year?"

Lenora's stomach toppled over itself sickeningly. She'd been ravenous five minutes ago, but now she doubted she could force a forkful of the sumptuous food down her throat.

Jason was leaving.

Within the week and he might be gone for a year. *A year. An entire year?* It seemed like a lifetime. And when he returned, would it be to England or America? To her? Or would he have forgotten Lenora by then?

Of course, she'd known this day was coming. She'd tried to prepare herself for it. Only...she'd hoped for... What? That he'd toss aside his career? Pledge undying love for her and forsake everything of his previous life to be with her?

Could she have done the same if Jason had asked it of her?

No. Lenora didn't think she could have. To leave England and her family never to return as Jason's mother had?

That knowledge nauseated her further.

If she was in love with Jason, wouldn't she forsake all else for him?

And him for you?

Even so, one of them would come out the loser in a contest neither desired.

Landry gave Jason a flinty look before shifting his attention to Lenora. His expression softened, and an apology lurked in his gray eyes.

Why was Landry putting Jason on the spot? Forcing his hand?

For the first time since Landry had found Lenora, genuine anger and outrage welled within her toward him.

How dare he?

She didn't need him interfering in matters of the heart. Did he doubt her intelligence? Her ability to discern a rogue from a gentleman. Jason mightn't be a polished aristocrat, but everything within her told her he was a decent, honorable man.

A man who women swarmed to.

Yes, he meant to sail to India. He'd never led Lenora to believe otherwise. Never implied he wouldn't carry on with his plans.

Had she just been a flirtation? Someone to amuse himself with until he sailed?

No. Of course not.

Are you positive? that maddening inner voice that wouldn't permit Lenora to deceive herself prodded.

That day in the park when Jason had kissed her surged to the forefront of her mind.

"Can you? Put down roots, that is?"

With a sinking heart and stomach, Lenora realized Jason hadn't answered her.

To disguise the hurt Landry's behavior caused and her chagrin at practically having thrown herself at Jason, Lenora cut a strawberry. "A sea captain does tend to sail from time to time, Landry. Just as lords sit in Parliament and a physician attends his patients. It's called responsibility."

She lifted her gaze to her brother's.

Landry visibly flinched at the accusation, and the hurt she knew must be shining in her eyes. She turned to Jason. "Thank you for the dance, Captain. I fear I'm feeling unwell all of a sudden and must beg your forgiveness."

Anything she forced down her throat would make an immediate reappearance.

Standing, she balanced her hands on the table. "Excuse me."

Celestia rose too. "Let me accompany you to the retiring room while Landry calls for our coach." She wrapped an arm around Lenora's waist. "Good evening, Captain Steele."

Lenora raised her head, positive her heartbreak shone in her eyes for all to see. This must end before it became even more difficult. Before this budding love for Jason became a conflagration she couldn't control.

So, she did what she ought to have done weeks ago—bid Jason *au dieu* once and for all.

"Goodbye, Captain."

The merest flexing of his eyes revealed he knew this wasn't simply a farewell for the evening. However, to make certain, Lenora swallowed the wad of tears tightening her throat. Averting her gaze because she couldn't bear to look into his beautiful hazel eyes and see her own heartbreak mirrored there, she said, "*Bon voyage* and God speed."

You're taking my heart with you, my love.

THIRTEEN

Aboard the Windswept Dream
East India Docks, London
23 December 1820
A quarter past eleven in the morning

From the poop deck, Jason ran a practiced eye across the bustling activity on the decks below. Everything was ship-shape, and the *Windswept Dream* was ready to weigh anchor with the tide in four days. Her crew was experienced, the first mate, capable and professional, and the ship was one of Stapleton Shipping and Supplies' finest.

Jason ought to be elated.

Instead, his mind returned to Lenora for the umpteenth time. He missed her. So much so that she was the first thing he thought of upon waking, and her name was on his lips when exhaustion finally lulled him to sleep in the early morning hours.

A permanent ache had taken up residence behind his breastbone in the vicinity of his heart. Was this what a broken heart felt like? Everything around him went on as before, except all of the joy had been sucked out of his life. He functioned in a fog, feeling only half alive.

Since the night of the ball, he'd sent Lenora a letter every day asking to see her. When the first several had gone unanswered, he'd delivered the last two notes in person only to be informed by Teeven in icy, condescending tones that she was not at home.

Not at home, Jason's arse.

"Please see that she receives this." Jason doubted Lenora would.

The intimidating butler had politely taken the letter Jason passed him before firmly shutting the door and leaving Jason standing awkwardly on the stoop.

Either she'd given orders not to receive him, or someone else had.

Keyworth. Interfering bounder.

Jason was positive Lenora felt something for him. He'd seen the way she looked at him, had tasted her sweet lips and vowed that he stirred a resonance in her soul as she did in his.

If she were behind Jason's chilly reception at Keyworth House, it was unlike her.

That had never been her way. Honest and direct, she'd always faced conflict with commendable fearlessness. Good God, she'd taken on two street youths to defend his grandmother. She would not cower from a simple conversation.

And yet, she'd clearly bid him goodbye the other night. Had she slammed a door in his face, her message couldn't have been more explicit.

You are free. Leave me be.

If Jason had an ounce of common sense, he'd leave her alone. He'd grant Lenora her desire to be done with him.

I cannot.

But he didn't believe that was what she really wanted. By

Jove, it wasn't what *he* wanted either. What she wanted was a man who she could trust to be by her side, not halfway across the world when she needed him.

The idea of sailing without seeing Lenora, without telling her what she meant to him, was akin to a draft horse's kick to Jason's gut. No, being run down by a fully laden freight wagon was more apt.

In the hope of meeting her, Jason had gone to Hyde Park every day, arriving well before eight and lingering until nine.

Lenora had never come.

Because she'd known he'd be there?

Did she feel betrayed that he hadn't told her when he was sailing? Did she feel as if he'd been playing with her affections these past weeks?

He should've told her about India, but the truth of it was that he wasn't eager to leave England. To leave her. What if she married while he was away?

No. By all that was holy, no! That notion was as untenable as lobster left too long in the sun.

In Jason's heart, Lenora was his.

He loved her.

Had loved her for weeks, but he hadn't been able to come to terms with the logistics of where they would live. He wouldn't be so cruel as to take her from a brother she'd only just come to know. Neither could Jason make England his permanent home. And even with the small fortune he'd amassed, it wasn't sufficient to live on for the rest of their lives.

He must have a means of income.

So, unable to contrive a solution, Jason had kept silent about his feelings for Lenora and the damnable pending voyage. Regardless, his honor had compelled him to tell Brockman weeks ago that there was a possibility he mightn't be able to accept the assignment.

Ronan had nodded slowly, his gaze keen with comprehension. "Miss Audsley?"

"Yes," was all Jason had admitted.

He wouldn't tell another what Lenora should hear first from him.

"I understand, Jason. Once I fell in love with Mercy, there was no question of me sailing anymore." Ronan had clapped Jason on the back.

Ronan made it sound so simple, but then again, he and his wife were both British.

"You have until the twenty-seventh to make a decision," Ronan said. "The *Windswept Dream's* first mate is perfectly capable of captaining the ship. I would like to give McCurdy a couple of days' notice of his promotion to captain if you decline to sail in the end."

When Lenora had continued to ignore Jason's attempts to contact her, uncertainty had assailed him. Mayhap she no longer felt the same way about him as he did her. Perhaps Keyworth had succeeded in planting doubts in her mind.

Swearing beneath his breath, he nodded to a pair of sailors coiling ropes and made his way to the quarter deck where Angus McCurdy—the first mate—was in conversation with the ship's surgeon.

Jason's parents had arrived in England two days ago.

His mother had taken one look at him and said, "Who is she?"

Jason shook his head, welcoming the steady wind lashing across his face. He'd told her about Lenora. About how conflicted he was. One part of him didn't want to leave her. Ever. The other couldn't imagine giving up sailing.

"Why must you do either?" Mama had asked, eyeing him over a cup of tea in Grandmother's old-fashioned salon. "If she loves you, she may very well want to sail with you. Have you asked her?"

Jason explained about Lenora's recent reunion with her brother and the earl's reluctance to be separated from her again. "I would never ask Lenora to choose, Mama. I'm confident she has no more wish to live in America than I do in England."

His mother made a comforting sound but didn't speak.

Hunching his shoulders, Jason had plowed a hand through his hair. "I don't know what to do. I would hate myself if Lenora was miserable."

Mama had tilted her head, a mysterious, knowing smile hovering around her mouth. "Darling, marriage is never either-or. It's a series of compromises and concessions, and when you add a deep abiding love to the mix, you'll find things often work themselves out."

"But you didn't see your parents for three decades."

Pouring tea into her cup, she nodded. "True." Mama glanced up, the blue rose adorned teapot still in her hand. "More tea?"

"No, thank you."

After adding two lumps of sugar and a dribble of milk, she stirred the contents of her cup. "I would've returned to England during that time had I ever been welcome, Jason. And, more on point, your father would've gladly accompanied me. In truth, now that my mother is widowed, I foresee us spending a great deal more time here. She's also expressed a desire to see America."

Jason had chuckled. "She's quite something, your mother."

Eyes twinkling, Mama laughed. "My mother is much more of a free spirit than I had ever imagined." She sobered and set her teacup down. "Jason, if you love Lenora, then you must find a way to tell her before you sail."

Jason picked up his pace, causing Mr. McCurdy to turn toward him with a question in his green eyes. By God, Jason couldn't—*wouldn't*—leave without seeing Lenora one last time. To ask her to be his wife and trust that love would, indeed, make a way.

"Mr. McCurdy?"

"Aye, Captain?"

"I'm off to propose to the woman I love. If she says yes, you'll be captaining the *Windswept Dream* to India."

FOURTEEN

Keyworth House
Mayfair, London
23 December 1820
Half of four

One hand holding the lace curtain to the side, Lenora turned from the bay window as Teeven entered the drawing room with a tea tray. Though Christmas was but two days away and nearly every room in Keyworth House had been beautifully decorated to celebrate the holiday, she couldn't summon an ounce of Christmas spirit.

"Come, Lenora," Mama coaxed, holding up a plate of gingerbread. Her bright smile didn't eliminate the troubled crease between her eyebrows. She was worried about Lenora. "I asked Mrs. Cox to make your favorite."

The mouth-watering aroma of warm gingerbread cake—spices and molasses—wafted across the room. Mama, Landry, and Celestia had done their utmost to lift her spirits since the ball when she'd bid Jason farewell.

She'd nearly blurted her love for him while they danced.

Thank God she had not.

Lenora still believed it was for the best that they go their separate ways. That didn't mean every breath didn't cause a stab of pain to her heart or that this was the first Christmas in her memory—even when she and Mama had been poor as paupers—that she didn't anticipate the holiday.

"I've heard whispers of a Frost Fair in January," Celestia said as Landry helped her onto the settee. The child within her grew, and she struggled to sit and stand, so large was her tummy.

"I have too." Giving her a stern look, he said, "You'll be permitted nothing more strenuous than a docile sleigh ride."

Landry took the seat beside his wife and snatched a Shrewsbury cake. He made short work of the sweet.

"Lenora, come away from the window. It's too cold," Mama prompted.

The temperature was biting, but they were snug inside the house, and the cold affected them little. Of late, Mama's protective tendencies had become almost cloying. More than once, Lenora had bitten her tongue against an urge to tell her mother to stop fussing so much. In a fortnight, she'd be one-and-twenty.

It was time Mama and Landry allowed her more autonomy. After all, if she was strong enough to permit the man she loved his freedom, then she was assuredly able to assert more independence.

Now, however, wasn't the time for that discussion. Not with Christmas looming in a couple of days. Marshaling a smile for the others, Lenora let the curtain fall into place once more. It was snowing again.

"You must permit me to teach you to skate."

Not so very long ago, she'd believed she and Jason might, somehow, make a life together. Foolish her. Jason had never declared himself. He'd been a charming and deucedly hand-some companion, and she'd foolishly imagined there was something more between them.

Even if there had been, Lenora loved Jason too much to ask him to give up his life upon the sea or live in England. His happiness meant more than her own.

She'd just settled onto the cushion beside her mother when a ruckus in the corridor had them all looking toward the drawing room's entrance.

"Are we expecting anyone for tea today, darling?" Landry asked Celestia.

Creases puckering her brow, she shook her head. "No. The weather is too foul for anyone with any sense to venture outdoors."

"I say, you cannot!" Teeven declared, just short of a bellow.

The distinct sound of flesh upon flesh filtered into the room.

What in heaven's name?

Her face pinched with worry, Mama brought a hand up to her neck. "Whatever is happen—?"

Jason burst through the doorway, fists balled, his coat disheveled, and his face flushed. His chest rose and fell swiftly, and he panted slightly as if he'd sprinted from the front of the house, up the stairs, and to the drawing room.

Halfway into the room, he swung about to face the door.

Teeven, sporting a bruised cheek and eyes flashing with outrage, charged inside. He stumbled to a stop upon seeing Lenora and the others gaping, open-mouthed.

Landry recovered first. Springing to his feet, he demanded, "Steele, what is the meaning of this?" He veered Teeven a side-ways glance. "Zounds. Did you *strike* my butler?"

Jason gave an unapologetic, terse nod. "I did. Knocked

him on his..." He speared the ladies a glance. "Uh...I knocked him down when he refused to admit me so that I might speak with Lenora."

Lenora wasn't positive, but there might've been a jot of admiration in Landry's expression. Teeven had been a prize-fighter in his prime. For Jason to have landed him a blow that sent him onto his bum meant he could hold his own in the ring.

With his build—those muscled thighs and broad shoulders—she wasn't surprised.

She also rose, glancing uncertainly between Jason and Landry and resisting the urge to fling herself into Jason's arms, pride be hanged.

"I beg your pardon, Teeven," Jason said. "I was desperate to see Lenora so that I can tell her I love her."

He looked directly at Lenora when he made the declaration, and the love in his hazel eyes made her pulse quicken even as her heart skipped a beat.

Someone gasped, but Lenora wasn't sure who.

It didn't matter.

Jason loved her.

He loved her.

Teeven's harsh features relaxed. Clearing his throat, he straightened his waistcoat and bowed his head minutely. "I confess, Captain Steele, your right jab is impressive."

His regard gravitated to Mama, and something unspoken passed between them.

Mama turned a ghastly shade of gray and clutched at her throat with one hand and wadded her serviette with the other.

Landry skirted the tea table. With a nod, he dismissed Teeven.

"Thank you, Teeven. That will be all. I shall ring if I require you."

"Very good, sir." The butler departed, closing the door behind him.

Astute man. He knew whatever was about to occur was better kept private.

"You might've sent a note round in advance, Steele, and requested an audience," Landry suggested, a hint of mockery and menace in his tone.

"I did. Every day, sometimes twice a day, for the past week." Jason's attention sidled to Lenora. "I personally delivered the last two letters only to be told Lenora was not at home."

"But I *was* at home." She hadn't even been permitted her walks in Hyde Park after Dottie had eloped with Mrs. March's footman the day after the Wimpletons' Christmas ball.

Forehead scrunched, Lenora pulled her focus from Jason and pinned Landry with an affronted glare. He stared back at her, his expression troubled.

"Really, Landry? You told Teeven to tell Jason I wasn't at home?" She planted her hands on her hips. "And where are the letters? I haven't seen a single one."

"I feared you didn't want to hear from me," Jason said, his gaze searching hers. "And that was why I'd had no response."

"And yet, here you are," Landry muttered drolly.

"Landry," Celestia admonished softly. "Be nice."

"I am always nice," he returned glibly.

Lenora was so angry that it was all she could do to keep from lashing out at her brother. He'd gone too far.

"Hmm? Have you nothing to say for yourself, Landry?" she demanded frostily.

Rubbing the end of his nose with a bent finger, he considered her for a long moment, then slid his gaze to Jason. "I never gave a directive to intercept letters from Steele to you,

Lenora. Nor did I give instructions to the staff to say you were not at home."

A bit of the starch went out of Lenora. "But if you didn't, who did?"

This made no sense.

"I did," Mama said in an unsteady voice. "I kept the letters from you."

<h1 style="text-align:center">FIFTEEN</h1>

"I didn't want the captain to take you away from me," Mama wept. "I knew you'd fallen in love with him, and one only has to look at Captain Steele to see he's mad about you too."

"Oh dear," Celestia murmured beneath her breath.

"Oh, Mama." Lenora sank to the settee and gathered her mother's hands in hers. "Surely you must know that wherever I go, you will too. Just like Ruth and Naomi. I would never leave you behind nor abandon you."

She raised her eyes to meet Jason's.

Smiling tenderly, he gave a slight nod.

Of course, he understood. He, above all others, had always understood her.

"Forgive me, Lenora." Her mother dabbed at the corner of her eye. "I was selfish. These last few days, I've seen how miserable you are." She sniffed and wiped her nose, then patted Lenora's face. "I want you to be happy, my dear. I shan't stand in the way any longer."

"And neither will I," Landry said, further astonishing Lenora.

From Jason's flummoxed countenance, her brother had taken him aback as well.

"You don't object anymore, Landry?" Lenora asked. "Why the change?"

"Anyone willing to toss aside my dire warnings to stay away from you and take on Teeven is a man who would do anything for you." A hint of sadness creased the corners of his eyes. "That's all I ever wanted for you, Lenora. It's what you deserve."

Celestia cleared her throat. "Yes, well. Why don't we give Lenora and Captain Steele a few moments of privacy?"

"Ten minutes," Landry conceded grudgingly, aiding his wife to her feet.

Jason canted his head in acknowledgment.

Mama rose too and offered Jason a wobbly smile. "Please forgive me, Captain Steele. I am not a vindictive woman by nature. I was afraid. Not a good excuse, but an honest one."

"Think no more on it, Mrs. Smith. Consider it already forgotten." He gave her a genial smile, and Lenora loved him all the more for his kindness. "You will always be welcome in our home."

"Thank you." Managing a weak upward tilt of her own mouth, Mama followed Landry and Celestia from the room.

The door closed with a soft snick.

Before the clock pendulum swung back and forth, Lenora was in Jason's arms.

~

"Lenora, my very own love." Jason buried his face in Lenora's hair. Honeysuckle and orange blossoms perfumed the satiny strands. "I almost made the worst mistake of my life."

His voice had gone ragged with emotion.

Trailing his lips from her ear to her jaw, he spoke between hot kisses. "As I stood on the *Windswept Dream's* deck, I realized a voyage anywhere wasn't what I wanted. You, Lenora Audsley, are all that I want. You are all that I need."

Her arms encircling his waist, Lenora angled her head away from his searching mouth.

"I love you too, Jason. So much that I was willing to let you go if that was what would make you happiest."

A groan throttled its way up his throat. "My unselfish, darling. That is so like you. But I can't imagine a life without you now. I don't want to contemplate such a dreary, lonely existence."

He swept his mouth over hers, gratified when she opened her lips for him. At once, Jason plunged his tongue inside the honeyed cavern of her mouth. She tasted of tea and spices.

A barely audible moan escaped Lenora as she arched into him.

Cupping her bottom, he pressed her belly into the evidence of his arousal. "See what you do to me, my love?"

A few moments later, Jason reluctantly lifted his head. "Your brother only gave me ten minutes, and I'm positive I've used up at least half of that allotted time already."

He sank to one knee.

Eyes brimming with joyous tears, Lenora gazed down at him, her face radiant with love. God, what had he done to deserve such a gift?

He fumbled in his pocket for a moment, then withdrew a simple gold band studded with blue diamonds. Holding it between his thumb and forefinger, Jason said, "The instant I saw the ring in the jeweler's, I knew it was perfect for you, darling. These rare blue diamonds are more turquoise than blue and are nearly the same color as your eyes."

"It's stunning, Jason." She gave him a tremulous smile and blinked rapidly. "I'm afraid you've made me quite emotional."

He took her hand and kissed the knuckles. "Lenora Esther Elizabeth Audsley, will you marry me? Be my partner and friend? Be my rudder on the ship of our lives together?"

"I want to say yes, Jason." She bit her lower lip, then laughed softly. "Rather desperately, in fact. But we haven't discussed where we'll live, and I fear it matters greatly."

Jason smiled up into her troubled face.

"We'll have homes in America and England. I've been offered a position with Stapleton Shipping and Supplies that I've accepted. It means no voyages to foreign ports. In essence, I would coordinate the operations between their United States offices and those in England. I would make semi-annual voyages between America and England."

This morning when he'd stopped by the offices of Stapleton Shipping and Supplies to inform them of his decision not to sail to India, a letter had been waiting for him with the offer. Evidently, Ronan Brockman had mentioned marriage might be in Jason's future the last time he spoke with Viscountess Sethwick.

The proposition was a godsend, in truth—an answer to a desperate prayer.

Jason intended to pen an acceptance if Lenora agreed to marry him.

A brilliant smile wreathed her face. "I can think of nothing that would make me happier than to become your wife, Jason."

He slipped the ring on her finger, then rose and drew her into his arms once more. "I think you'll enjoy sailing. You have an adventurous spirit, though it hasn't been given free rein."

"I was afraid to love you, Jason. Afraid you were a rogue who would break my heart."

"I vow before God, Lenora, you'll never have cause to doubt me. I have never loved another. In fact, I doubted true love existed. Until you."

Sighing, she nestled closer. "I'll remember this as the best Christmas ever."

Tilting her chin upward, Jason lowered his mouth to hers once more.

What could Keyworth do if he came upon them?

Insist they marry by a special license?

Excellent.

"And you are the greatest gift I'll ever receive, my darling."

EPILOGUE

Aboard The Arcturus
Atlantic Ocean
Captain's Cabin
25 June 1822

Not ready to awaken just yet, Lenora sighed, snuggling deeper into the cozy blankets. The crossing from Massachusetts to England had been colder than last time. She loved this time of day when the ship was just rousing, and the cabin rocked back and forth.

As it turned out, Lenora was an excellent sailor. Seasickness didn't plague her, which had come as a most welcome surprise. It seemed she had a hardy constitution because she didn't suffer from morning sickness either.

"Good morning, my love," Jason murmured in her ear, the rough stubble of his beard scraping the back of her neck.

"Good morning," she murmured, starting to turn over.

He stayed her movement with a palm to her hip as he swept the hair off her neck and shoulders with his other hand.

Dropping light kisses along her shoulder and nape, he trailed a hand over her buttocks.

As always, his touch turned her to melted wax, and Lenora arched into him, pressing her bottom into the stiff member probing between her thighs.

"I meant to wake you to see if you wanted to catch the first glimpse of England's shoreline in the distance," he murmured before nipping her shoulder.

A shudder of desire winged through her.

"That would be nice," she managed on a gasp as he ventured his hand lower. "It's rather poignant." Especially since her mother had stayed in England the last voyage. Not only was she a poor sailor, but she and Teeven had also married.

The union had quite taken everyone by surprise.

"We'll have to hurry." Jason's leisurely exploration belied any need to rush.

"Well, don't hesitate on my behalf." Lenora gyrated her hips in invitation.

With a half chuckle, half growl, Jason accepted her offer. As the ship rose and fell, so did they in a rhythm as old as time itself.

As Lenora crested the peak, an instant before she came utterly undone, she cried, "I love you."

Jason's guttural response was lost as he buried his face in the crook of her neck and found his own release.

Breathing heavily, she turned onto her side to face him. Placing a palm on his cheek, Lenora kissed her husband, relishing the rub of his bristly face against hers. The babe kicked, and as her tummy was pressed against his, Jason felt their child's movement.

His eyes went wide as they lashed to hers and then to Lenora's stomach. Grinning, he lay his palm flat over the mound. "Do you think it's a boy or a girl?"

"Yes. I'm sure it is."

"Minx."

Lenora giggled when Jason tickled her ribs.

The baby moved again, and they both laid their hands on her distended belly. "I'm glad we'll be in England for the child's birth. I want my mother present for the occasion." Lenora raised her gaze to Jason's. "She's never seen a birth."

"That may be so, but Ruth does not lack grandmotherly instincts." Jason kissed her forehead. "Keyworth said she dotes on Levi."

"I think Landry and Celestia appreciate her. Their mothers aren't alive, so Mama is the closest thing Levi has to a grandmother."

Jason rose up on one elbow. "I ask myself every day why God has blessed me with you as a wife." He trailed a finger down her jaw. "I would've given it all up for you, Lenora. Sailing, captaining ships, living in America. All of it."

"I know you would have done." Lifting her head, Lenora brushed her mouth against his. "And I couldn't let you. True love gives. It doesn't take."

"And I shall give you my unfailing love, even after I leave this earth, my darling wife."

If you'd like to leave a review, I would be grateful.

Keep reading for a free preview of
A ROGUE WORTH THE RISK
The Honorable Rogues®
Book Eight

Nottingshire Court
Home of Lady Pandora Osborne
Essex, England
Middle of January — Evening

I shouldn't have come.

This was a monumental mistake. A sodding, imbecilic, bloody mistake.

Putting two fingers to the jagged scar zigzagging across his left cheek, Caspian Graystone, Baron Strathmore—called the blackhearted baron behind his back and occasionally to his face—paused inside the ballroom's glittering entrance.

Why had he allowed Ronan Brockman and Manchester, Marquess of Sterling, to talk him into attending what was certain to be a week-long, excruciatingly tedious pain in the posterior? Cynicism bent Caspian's mouth upward, and anyone glancing in his direction would recognize him for what he was—a jaded, sardonic skeptic.

Elegantly coiffed ladies draped in sparkling jewels and swathed in silks and satins in every shade of the rainbow twirled around the chalked parquet dance floor with gentlemen attired in the first stare of fashion.

Pretentious popinjays and conceited coxcombs, the lot.

Nay, not all of the fellows.

According to Brockman, a few other sensible chaps made the coveted guest list, though how Brockman came by that exclusive information was anyone's guess. The Earls of Hythe, Bixley, and Barington, as well as Viscounts Harcourt, Silverton, and the Duke of Sedgewick were expected. Whether the lords chose to subject themselves to this gratuitous torment or not, however...

They were the only thing that kept Caspian from turning on his heel and sequestering himself for the evening in the study or library with a bottle of prime scotch. Mayhap not a bottle, but a dram or two.

In truth, the notion tempted greatly.

Though an aristocrat by birthright, Caspian didn't belong here—didn't belong amongst *le beau monde*. The *ton* had made that perfectly clear six years ago. Regardless, he'd made his friends a promise, and if nothing else—despite the smudges upon his dented reputation—Caspian was a man of his word.

In point of fact, just appearing tonight would suffice as the fulfillment of his pledge to attend the house party. No need to torture himself and stay more than a day or two.

Besides, he preferred to monitor Thirkwick Park's reconstruction progress himself. He'd far rather be there laying bricks, hoisting lumber, nailing flooring, or performing any number of other tasks required to rebuild the once-magnificent manor that had sustained grievous fire damage.

The very inferno Caspian had escaped by diving through an upper-story window—hence his scarred face and arm. The blaze had also taken the lives of his entire family: father, brother, pregnant sister-in-law, and demented stepmother, Florinda. Caspian would go to his grave convinced Florinda had set the fire in one of her frequent and ever more irrational frenzies.

With pure determination, he took a firm grip on his memory and veered his disquieting musings from that fateful night. With bored disinterest, he surveyed the festive tableau before him. The merest pinch of a headache throbbed behind his eyes as it inevitably did when he entertained recollections of the deadly conflagration that had left him alone in the world.

The fire that had also left Caspian a pariah to Society.

In an effort to ease the aggravating ache prodding his skull, Caspian rubbed the bridge of his nose. He stopped as two ladies passed, their eyes widening in recognition, before they dipped their graying heads together. The feathers in their silk turbans battled for dominance in a comical duel as the women broke into frenetic whispers.

Indulging the wicked urge to take them down a peg, Caspian gave them a devilish wink and skewed his mouth into a mocking grin. He knew full well that his scar pulled his mouth into a cockeyed, rather macabre grimace. More than one child had broken into frightened cries when he'd smiled at them.

So he'd stopped doing so.

He might be a monster in appearance but wasn't so in character. Unless one counted cynicism and taciturnity as character flaws.

Clutching one another's arms in alarm, the be-ribboned and be-ruffled dames practically fell over each other in their haste to put distance between him and them. It would serve the biddies right if they toppled, ample bosoms over even ampler bums, onto the dance floor.

Though he was loath to admit it, the encounter bothered Caspian more than it ought. Hadn't his pride been bludgeoned enough? Why put himself through this farce?

He searched the teeming ballroom for a single friend. He hadn't many left, truth be told. Merely a handful of loyal men who valued character over rumors. Friendship over titillating tattle. Who believed him and not the embellished gossip still circulating certain elite drawing rooms.

To be perfectly honest, the invitation to attend Lady Pandora Osborne's house party had taken him aback. They didn't travel in the same social circles, although she had been a close friend of his mother's many long years ago.

Perhaps pity or a misguided sense of obligation had spurred her to include Caspian. A perverted sense of curiosity or anticipation his presence would liven up an otherwise predictable gathering weren't farfetched motivations either.

In retrospect, the latter two were the more likely possibilities.

Barely suppressing a peeved sigh, Caspian pulled his watch from his pocket.

Not even ten of the clock yet.

Where was Brockman? Sterling?

Had they deserted him this early on?

Caspian skimmed his gaze across the crowd again. Hundreds of candles in the crystal chandeliers cast an ethereal glow onto the guests, creating a fairytale-like atmosphere.

Fairytale?

Balderdash and twaddle.

He'd put aside fanciful childish notions twenty years ago. When his invalid mother had died, and Father had married Florinda—the unbalanced mistress he'd unabashedly flaunted —less than a fortnight later.

There wasn't anything magical or mystical about the

people gathered at Lady Osborne's ostentatious manor house. With few exceptions, the guests were shopping the Marriage Mart, hunting matrimonial prey, or intent on engaging in a clandestine assignation—perchance more than one naughty tryst.

A derisive snort escaped Caspian.

Heaven save him from such obvious machinations.

The bachelor's life suited him very well.

Very well, indeed, thank you.

He felt no pressing need to sire an heir—no need at all, in point of fact. As the second son, that task wasn't ever to have been his responsibility. Which was why —even as the barony's heir—he'd never entertained notions of marching down the aisle and voluntarily relinquishing his freedom for matrimonial imprisonment.

"Ah, there you are, Strathmore."

A sharp swat to his arm brought his attention to the formidable lady attired in black whose silent approach he'd missed.

His daunting hostess.

"I didn't believe you'd actually come." Lady Pandora Osborne, Pansy to her closest friends, scraped a probing gaze over him through her lorgnette. "Although Sterling assured me you would."

"My lady." Caspian dutifully bent into a bow. "A delight."

Though the silver curls artfully arranged upon her noble head scarcely reached Caspian's shoulders, Lady Osborne was a force to be reckoned with. A veritable dervish when she put her mind to something. Her ladyship was also the *ton's* most prestigious unofficial matchmaker and was renowned for her brilliant matches.

An aptitude she took tremendous pride in.

Toying with the lace edging her hand-painted fan, she eyed him critically then gave an approving nod.

Evidently, Caspian had measured up. To what, he wasn't certain.

"You clean up well, Strathmore. Black suits you."

What else would the Blackhearted Baron wear?

Lady Osborne artfully swept a hand from her neck to waist. "I favor the shade myself."

Neither apologetic nor contrite, she shifted her bold scrutiny to his disfigured face, and Caspian raised a sardonic eyebrow.

"Even with that scar." She pointed her fan at his disfigured cheek. "You're more handsome than either your brother or father were."

"High praise indeed from one as estimable as yourself, my lady."

"Pshaw. Poppycock." She cut him a teasing glance, humor twinkling in her eyes. "Don't waste your glib tongue on me, rapscallion."

Her gaze took on a cunning gleam, and Caspian had the distinct impression she was up to something. Something he wasn't going to like.

"There are plenty of young ladies who would swoon for an opportunity to dance with you tonight, Strathmore."

I hope you enjoyed this free preview of
A ROGUE WORTH THE RISK
***The Honorable Rogues*®**
Book Eight

FROM THE DESK OF COLLETTE CAMERON®

Thank you for reading 'TWAS THE ROGUE BEFORE CHRISTMAS, The Honorable Rogues® Book Seven. If you enjoyed the story, please consider leaving a review.

I first put Jason Steele on the page in NO LADY FOR THE LORD as Ronan Brockman's best friend. My readers were very intrigued with Lenora when they read about her in EARL OF KEYWORTH and asked me to give Lenora her own story. As it sometimes happens with my characters, I knew instantly that Lenora Audsley would be Jason's soul mate.

In an interesting twist that I hadn't planned, but Jason and Lenora's story led me there, 'TWAS THE ROGUE BEFORE CHRISTMAS mentions characters from four of my other series. If you are interested in learning more about them, their stores are listed below.

Allen and Olivia Wimpleton – A KISS FOR A ROGUE, The Honorable Rogues® series

Ronan and Mercy Brockman – NO LADY FOR THE LORD, Secrets of Scandalous Ladies series

Chance and Ivy Faulkenhurst – A BRIDE FOR A ROGUE, The Honorable Rogues® series

Pierce, Earl of Wainthorpe – EARL OF WAINTHORPE, For the Love of an Earl series (Wicked Earls' Club)

Landry and Celestia Audsley, Earl and Countess of Keyworth – EARL OF KEYWORTH, For the Love of an Earl series (Wicked Earls' Club)

Ewan and Yvette McTavish, Viscount and Viscountess Sethwick – THE HIGHLANDER'S HEIRESS, Highland Heather Romancing a Scot: Castle Brides series

If you'd like to read the story where Sampson plays matchmaker, you'll find the full account in NEVER DANCE WITH A DUKE, Dukes Come Calling Series.

To stay abreast of the releases of my other books, you can subscribe to my newsletter (the link is below) or visit my author world at collettecameron.com.

I hope your escape into the romantic past with Jason and Lenora, when times were simpler and chivalry reigned, provided you with an enjoyable reprieve for a little while.

Hugs,
Collette

If you haven't joined Collette's exclusive mailing list click on QR image to sign up! You'll get access to exclusive content, sneak peeks, contests, giveaways, and more...
(P.S. No spam!)

https://collettecameronbooks.com/freegift

**Collette loves to hear from readers.
You can contact her via her website: collettecameron-books.com.
Or email her directly at collette@collettecameron-books.com.**

**You can also follow Collette on social media:
Facebook:** https://www.-facebook.com/ColletteCameronNovels/
Instagram: https://instagram.com/collettecameronauthor/
Goodreads: https://www.goodreads.com/collettecameron
Book Bub: https://www.bookbub.com/authors/collette-cameron

Pinterest: http://www.pinterest.com/colletteauthor/
YouTube: https://www.youtube.com/@ColletteCamero-nAuthor

Giggles are Guaranteed
Collette's Cheris Reader Group

https://www.facebook.com/groups/CollettesCheris/

If you love to chat about all things romance-book related and enjoy taking part in fun and engaging live events, contests, and giveaways join **Collette's Chèris VIP Reader Group, https://www.facebook.com/groups/CollettesCheris/,** my exclusive private book group on Facebook.

Giggles are guaranteed!

Hope to see you there,
Collette Cameron®

COLLETTE CAMERON®

USA Today Bestselling author Collette Cameron® is renowned for her captivating, humorous, and heartwarming Scottish and Regency historical romance novels. With over 65 published titles, over 1.6 million books sold around the world, and multiple writing awards to her credit, Collette is a well-known author in the world of historical romance.

Readers love her witty and relatable characters including daring rogues, dashing scoundrels, and the strong and spirited heroines who capture their hearts. From the rugged highlands to the refined drawing rooms of Regency England, Collette's novels will transport you to another time and place, where love and adventure are just a page away.

Collette's Sweet-to-Spicy Timeless Romances® are the perfect escape for readers looking for romantic escape, poignant inspiration, engaging humor, and entertaining stories.

Based in the Pacific Northwest, Collette is surrounded by the lush greenery and rainy skies that inspire her writing. She dreams of one day splitting her time between the Pacific Northwest and Scotland. In the meantime, she indulges in her love of all things cobalt blue, dachshunds, chocolate, and of course, crafting her next historical romance.

Blue Rose Romance® LLC
collette@collettecameronbooks.com
collettecameronbooks.com

ALSO BY COLLETTE CAMERON®

BLUE ROSE ROMANCE® LLC
COLLETTE CAMERON'S® COMPLETE BOOK LIST

CHRONICLES OF THE WESTBROOK BRIDES
A Romantic Opposites Attract Mystery & Suspense
Family Saga Regency Romance

Midnight Christmas Waltz — Book 1
Mission at Midnight — Book 2
The Midnight Marquess — Book 3
Holly, Mistletoe, and Midnight Snow — Book 4
The Wallflower's Midnight Waltz— Book 5
Minuet at Midnight— Book 6
Kiss a Rake at Midnight — Book 7
Unmasked at Midnight — Book 8
Memories Made at Midnight — Book 9
Once Upon a Midnight Dream — Book 10

DUKES COME CALLING
A Sensual Marriage of Convenience
Regency Historical Romance

A Diamond for a Duke — Book 1
Only a Duke Would Dare — Book 2

A December with a Duke — Book 3

What Would a Duke Do? — Book 4

Wooed by a Wicked Duke — Book 5

Duchess of His Heart — Book 6

Never Dance with a Duke — Book 7

Wedding Her Christmas Duke — Book 8

The Debutante and the Duke — Book 9

Loved by a Dangerous Duke — Book 10

How to Win a Duke's Heart — Book 11

When a Duke Desires a Lass — Book 12

My Dearest Duke — Book 13

~

FOR THE LOVE OF AN EARL (Wicked Earls' Club)
A Humorous Aristocrat and Wallflower
Regency Romance Adventure

Earl of Wainthorpe — Book 1

Earl of Scarborough — Book 2

Earl of Keyworth — Book 3

Earl of Renshaw — Book 4

~

HEART OF A SCOT
A Passionate Enemies to Lovers
Scottish Highlander Historical Mystery
Romance Adventure

To Love a Highland Laird — Book 1

To Redeem a Highland Rogue — Book 2

To Seduce a Highland Scoundrel — Book 3

To Woo a Highland Warrior — Book 4

To Enchant a Highland Earl — Book 5

To Defy a Highland Duke — Book 6

To Marry a Highland Marauder — Book 7

To Bargain with a Highland Buccaneer — Book 8

A Christmas Kiss for the Highlander — Book 9

~

HIGHLAND HEATHER ROMANCING A SCOT: CASTLE BRIDES

A Passionate Enemies to Lovers Second Chance

Scottish Highlander Mystery Romance

Heart of a Highlander — Prequel

The Viscount's Vow — Book 1

The Highlander's Heiress — Book 2

The Earl's Enticement — Book 3

Triumph and Treasure — Book 4

Virtue and Valor — Book 5

Heartbreak and Honor — Book

Scandal's Splendor — Book 7

Passion and Plunder — Book 8

Wishes and Wonder — Book 9

A Yuletide Highlander — Book 10

The Lord and the Wallflower — Book 3

The Buccaneer and the Bluestocking — Book 4

The Lieutenant and the Lady — Book 5

THE HONORABLE ROGUES®
A Second Chance Redeemable Rogue
and Wallflower Regency Romance

A Kiss for a Rogue — Book 1

A Bride for a Rogue — Book 2

A Rogue's Scandalous Wish — Book 3

To Capture a Rogue's Heart — Book 4

The Rogue and the Wallflower — Book 5

A Rose for a Rogue — Book 6

'Twas the Rogue Before Christmas — Book 7

A Rogue Worth the Risk — Book 8

www.ingramcontent.com/pod-product-compliance
Lightning Source LLC
Chambersburg PA
CBHW072138300726
48975CB00003B/1119